MURDER

OR

PESTLE?

To Kathy—
Thanks for your
Friendship &
support —

Best Wishes
&
Happy Reading—
Scott Mies

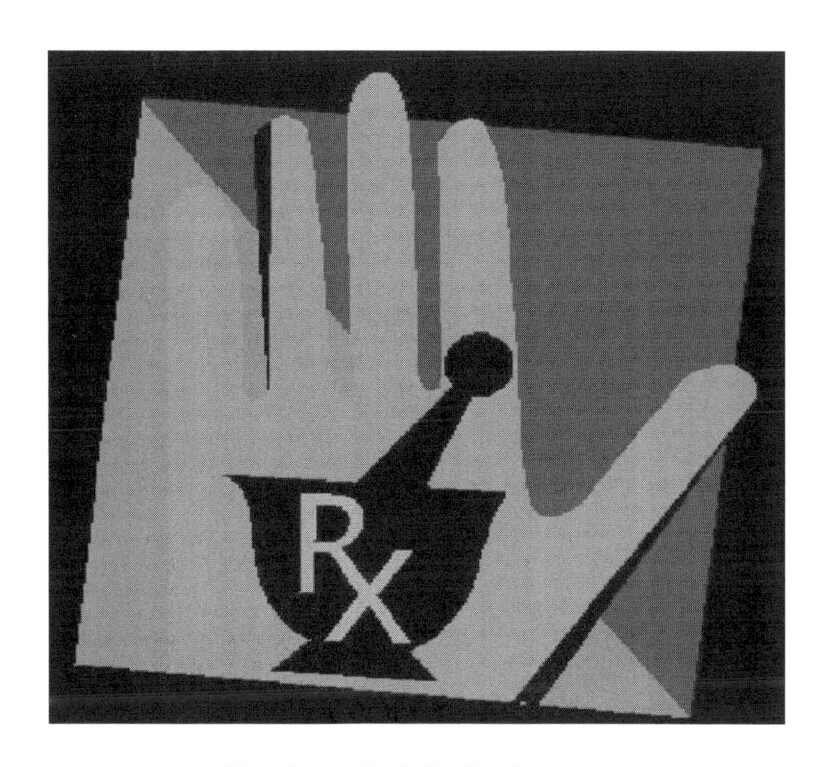

MURDER OR PESTLE?

BY

SCOTT MIES AND AL LODWICK

Printed in the United States of America

Second Edition: September 2013

10 9 8 7 6 5 4 3 2 1

Library of Congress Cataloging-in-Publication Data

Mies, Scott.
Lodwick, Al.

Murder or Pestle? / Scott Mies and Al Lodwick. – second ed.
p. cm.

ISBN-13: 978-0989775106

ISBN-10: 0989775100

Scott:

To Gwyneth, of course.

Al:

To my wife, Ann, whose encouragement and suggestions made this book possible.

Acknowledgments:

The authors wish to thank the following for their considerable contributions:

Ann Lodwick for her skillful editing.

Clay Loudon for book formatting and creative cover ideas.
clayton.loudon@gmail.com

Denise Elfenbein, Stellar Photography for authors photo.
(stellarphoto@hotmail.com)

Rachel Lodwick for company logo design.

Author's Biographies

Scott Mies is a retired educator with an "addiction" to murder mysteries and courtroom dramas. Scott is actively involved with the Prescott, Arizona community as a volunteer, "Big Brother," chorus member, and anything else he can check off his "bucket list." Mr. Mies continues to pursue his passion as a free-lance writer.

Al Lodwick is a retired pharmacist, living in Prescott, Arizona whose career spanned the era from compounding prescriptions to clinical pharmacy. Al served in Vietnam as an Army pharmacist. He managed "warfarin" and taught seminars on its proper use. Mr. Lodwick has served as an expert witness and litigation consultant in many legal actions.

1

Wednesday, July 26, 2000
Delmarva, a small town in Challenger County,
between Norfolk, VA and Baltimore, MD

A devastated Jeanette Linn, the sole passenger in her beloved automobile, a 1998 Cadillac Eldorado, was being driven home from the hospital by her neighbor and friend, Virgie Meade-Worthington. While the car was uninteresting beige gray, its sheer size and price tag rattled most of the locals in Delmarva and the greater Challenger County area.

Virgie was Jeanette's only real friend. The Linns, as all people who didn't grow up in Delmarva, were said to be from *away*, and were simply called *aways* by the town folks. It was next to impossible for an outsider to be accepted as extended kin in this small coastal town that was mostly populated with citizens who shared one of three last names: Tipsword, Meade, or Pickett. Fifty-six-year-old Virgie was born a Meade, then was briefly married to a transient fisherman who liked others to call him "Mr. Worthington." He often ranted that he was ready to captain his own fishing boat but that nobody would back him financially. In the end, he skipped town, broke Virgie's heart and left her with nothing more than his last name. For reasons unclear even to Jeanette Linn, Virgie retained the scoundrel's last name even though she divorced him for spousal abandonment over twenty-five years ago. She did, however, keep her maiden name by hyphenating it with Worthington, and made sure that Meade came first. Jeanette suspected that her friend felt that Virgie Meade-Worthington sounded more respectable as it indicated that she is or had been married, and not a spinster.

Although Virgie had lived in Delmarva all of her life and was a blood relative of about a third of the town's citizens, she tried to remain neutral about local politics. She also kept a low profile regarding her friendship with the *away*, Jeanette Linn.

A few days before it was Virgie who first told Jeanette that her son, Todd Linn (a.k.a. "Toddler") was in the intensive care unit at the Neptune General Medical Center. Now Jeanette was riding back from the hospital, having just given the doctors permission to "pull the plug" on her son, her only son, her only family.

Jeanette Linn had lost her husband, Frank to heart disease just two years before, and acknowledging that at age sixty-seven her own health was rapidly declining, she felt a chill of fear, yet resolve surge through her body.

"I hate that they call him the 'case' or the 'deceased.' He's my son! Nobody cares about Todd. Not the hospital, not the doctors, and for sure, not the almighty Challenger County Sheriff George Pickett," said Jeanette, sobbing with grief.

Minutes after Jeanette had signed the legal paperwork to take Todd off life support the sheriff had uttered, "What's done is done," which served as empty words of sympathy and a not-so-thinly-veiled message that the case was closed in his mind.

Todd Rayfield Linn was officially pronounced dead twenty minutes later. An autopsy was performed later that day. The medical cause of death was a brain hemorrhage.

"I want to know what happened, everything that happened. And I want justice for my son," rasped Jeanette, choking back tears.

After a few dangling moments of silence, Virgie said, "Give the sheriff and the deputies time to investigate, Jeanette. I know you're hurting badly. You must be dying inside, but what else can you do?"

Virgie looked over at Jeanette, who shook her head in response, then sat up straight in her seat and stared out through the front windshield. It looked to Virgie that Jeanette was praying, and, with nothing more to lose, was probably plotting her own form of justice. Jeanette had indeed been praying and plotting, not to break the law, but to give it a colossal nudge. More importantly, she had been trying to remember a name. "Alex Mann! Of course. I've got to call Alex Mann. I wonder if he's still in Arizona. Prescott, I think."

Virgie was trying her best to concentrate on her driving while following Jeanette's monologue. "Is this Mann guy a lawyer?"

"No," Jeanette replied, still looking straight ahead, "Remember when we first met, I told you about the burglary at our drug store out west?" Virgie nodded, then stopped more suddenly than she would've liked to for a stale yellow traffic light. Jeanette continued, "Well, he was our investigative pharmacy inspector in Arizona. We became better acquainted while he was working on the investigation. He cared; he was good; not like a lot of your law enforcement types. I hope he's still working. It's been a few years since I saw him. He's got a knack for finding out things. People talk to Alex even when they don't want to at first, and I'm desperately going to need his help."

Prescott (pronounced "Preskit" by the locals) is a small, mile-high city in Northern Arizona, about ninety miles north of Phoenix. Its population grew considerably over the years, and today is just under forty thousand residents. Despite the growth, people say Prescott still maintains its small-town feel and has lived up to its slogan, "Everybody's Home Town." Prescott has a rich history as a true town of the Wild West and was the first capital of the Arizona Territory in 1864.

Legendary characters like Wyatt Earp and Doc Holiday frequented the Palace Saloon and other drinking establishments on Prescott's infamous "Whiskey Row." The city has served as the backdrop for many westerns, including "How the West Was Won," "Junior Bonner," and "The Badlanders."

Alex had been a pharmacist for ten years in Pueblo, Colorado, and while he was not unhappy with his position, he was eager to take on new career challenges. When there was an opening for a Prescott-based Arizona State Board of Pharmacy Inspector, Alex and his wife, Betty, visited the city to see if they wanted to move there.

They were told by local residents they met that the temperatures were usually moderate, but they would experience all four seasons and even some snow. This was appealing to the Manns because they weren't keen on living in the extreme heat of the

Valley. They loved the city so much that they bought a wonderful old house with unobstructed views of awe-inspiring sunsets over Thumb Butte, a local landmark. Their home was just a few miles south of downtown, and they were forever charmed with the events held in the Courthouse Square.

Alex took this "some" snow information to heart and along with his and Betty's other prize possessions, they brought their snow blower on the move from Pueblo.

The Manns arrived in Prescott a few weeks before Christmas, 1989. The neighbors got downright delight in teasing Alex about hauling his contraption across state lines. "Besides," they declared, "it doesn't snow very much, and even when it does, it melts in a day or two."

About a month later, Prescott was hit with a moderate six-inch snowstorm. Alex saw shadows of figures peering out of the windows of his neighbors' homes as his snow blower almost effortlessly tore through the snow and shot it out harmlessly on either side of his steep, winding driveway. After finishing his own snow removal, Alex moved on and cleared the driveways of his neighbors on either side, directly across the road, and a neighbor's driveway around the bend where a ninety-four-year-old disabled military veteran lived.

As Alex staggered, cold and exhausted, back to his home, a small group of neighbors had gathered in a semi-circle around his mailbox and cheered as he came into view. With pride, Alex straightened his back and walked tall as he approached them. When they asked him if he was tired, Alex replied, "Not really, I've got technology in my shovel." They extended their arms to hand him coffee, hot chocolate, green tea, and a small silver flask of what smelled like whiskey. Alex thought:

"Now what about this contraption?" He smiled to himself and let his deeds do the talking.

Alex Everly Mann intentionally includes his middle name as a conversation starter when he introduces himself. People often ask him if his parents chose his middle name from the Everly Brothers. "No," he'll smile and reply, "I was born way before they got famous." This will, without fail, lead to further discussions about the group, the music of the 1950s, how Don and Phil Everly influenced many of today's singers, and the inevitable question, "By the way, are they still alive?"

Bearing a striking resemblance to a middle-age Ernest Hemingway, Alex has a ruddy face and an imposing white beard that he grows out or trims short at whim. Alex is even fond of wearing roll neck sweaters a'la Papa, not for ego, but as homage to one of his all-time favorite authors.

He was originally from a forgettable small town in Iowa. Alex was an only child, and his doting parents were hard-working yet mostly unsuccessful entrepreneurs. The family traveled around the country trying out new ventures, and although he never told his mother and father, Alex believed that Cher's hit song, "Gypsies, Tramps and Thieves" could have been the soundtrack for his childhood years. It may have seemed that way to a boy looking for a more stable home life, but Alex always had clean clothes, a proper bed and enough food to sustain him. Among his favorite family stints was their short-term ownership and management of a restaurant; a diner actually, located near an on-off ramp of a highway near San Antonio, Texas.

After school and on weekends, he would sit for hours in the diner's "owners' booth" near the kitchen or on the far end bar stool of the lunch counter. Amidst the chatter of competing conversations, he would tune into the patrons' travel tales, news and sports tidbits, and endless differences of opinion. Alex attributes his refined gift of gab and attentive listening skills to the two years he spent hanging around the diner. He has remained an avid traveler who prides himself on knowing where to get the best food with the biggest portions. He also knows the locations of the cleanest and most accessible restrooms throughout the U.S.

In the late 1950s, Alex was an easily-impressed teenager and had been visiting his aunt and uncle in Boston. They took him to visit the home of a prominent local pharmacy owner. The lady of the house had told her guests that she considered herself to be just an average American who flew to Bermuda for a vacation twice a year and tried to get to New York for shopping once a month. That's when Alex decided that he would like to become an "average American" and vowed to go to pharmacy school. In time, he also decided that he liked the wide open spaces of the West better than the congestion of the East.

Alex likes to trade off wearing one of the several Vietnam Veteran caps he owns. He wears them with pride. He had earned the right to wear them, and he soon learned that they were also another terrific conversation starter.

With military action rapidly escalating in Vietnam, Alex was drafted in the United States Army on December 7, 1966; the twenty-fifth anniversary of the bombing of Pearl Harbor. Friends joked that drafting Alex was the worst thing to happen to the U.S. military since that infamous event in 1941. He had spent eighteen months stateside, working as a pharmacist at Brooke General Hospital in San Antonio, Texas, and then was then sent to Vung Tau, South Vietnam to serve as a pharmacist with the 345th General Medical Dispensary. Although the patients and staff were not subject to ground action, they experienced occasional rocket attacks and could hear the distant rumble of U.S. Air Force B-52s on nightly bombing raids.

Friends ask him, "Why do you always wear your vet caps?"

"Because vets need to talk," says Alex, and he's right. He's greeted in stores, parks and restaurants by strangers who often salute, or nodded knowingly, or say, "Welcome home, Brother." But most of all, they want to talk – need to talk – about *then* and about *now*, but mostly about *then*.

Alex's intended quick shopping trips often run twice as long as planned because the veteran cap is working its magic like Dr. Brokaw's colorful apparel in Ray Bradbury's short story, "The Man in the Rorschach Shirt." Each vet has opinions, views on life, and a need to be heard. Alex's ability to disarm even the most wary human beings is a gift which serves him well in gathering information not available to less charming and engaging individuals.

2

September, 1996 - February, 1997
Clarkwood, a small town in Northern Arizona

Jeanette Linn and her husband, Frank originally met Alex in Clarkwood, Arizona on the morning of September 5, 1996; the day after Labor Day. Clarkwood has slightly less than three thousand residents and is, traffic permitting, about an hour's drive northeast of Prescott. Their meeting wasn't by chance and wasn't social in nature, although, over the next few weeks, Alex and the Linns would become friends.

The afternoon before, three events occurred in the small town that were connected only by timing and circumstances. The first and most obvious event on Monday, September 4, was the Labor Day celebration that included the eight o'clock pancake breakfast and the ten- thirty parade. It was a holiday on which most people were off work and in a celebratory state of mind.

Mayor Bart "King" Cotton decided to capitalize on the festive mood already established earlier that day by hosting the second main event in Clarkwood. He and his wife had invited the whole town to attend the wedding reception of their only daughter, Benita "Buffy" Cotton and Troy Mandarich. Buffy tried to picture how her married name would look on her new driver's license: Benita Louise Cotton-Mandarich. She frowned. It sounded choppy – not flowing, not lilting –

but she loved Troy, and most of the time she would simply be called Buffy.

The celebration was to be held in the town's quaint but impressive railroad station park, and when it was over the happy wedding couple would chug off into the sunset in their custom decorated and well-appointed caboose.

Mayor Cotton had wisely scheduled the affair to begin at two o'clock and end at four-thirty; after lunch and before dinner. In all fairness, there were tables abundantly scattered throughout the property loaded with tasty finger foods, a dozen tables laden with sweets and fifteen beverage stations complete with pitchers of lemonade, ice tea, soft drinks, and beer.

Around three o'clock, the wedding cakes – enough to give a small piece to each of the three thousand revelers – were served. The party also offered live music and dancing at a few locations around the train station. Security was tight for the gala event and every law enforcement person; including police, rent-a-cops, and deputized citizens were on hand. This localized security contributed to the third event in Clarkwood that day, and which may not have occurred had it been a normal day: The Linn Pharmacy Burglary.

The Linn Pharmacy – formerly known as Clarkwood Drugs and before that, simply Drug Store – was located downtown along the main street, Center Road. It was a large two-story red brick building flanked on the left by Downtown Dry Cleaners and on the right by Clarkwood Hardware.

The actual pharmacy was about four thousand square feet; counting the storage room below, which covered an area about the size of the Ear & Eye,

Dental Care, and Seasonal Products aisles. The second floor of the building consisted of two one-bedroom apartments; the larger of the two was occupied by Jeanette and Frank Linn, the smaller by their twenty-eight-year-old son, Todd Rayfield Linn.

Most of the citizens in Clarkwood somewhat good-naturedly called Todd, “Toddler,” since he was anything but. He was six feet eight inches tall but weighed less than one hundred sixty pounds. He had deep-set brown, almost black eyes and moved his body clumsily. He hunched over when he walked as if to level his height with those he shyly encountered. In spite of his stature, Todd was almost invisible in high school. Todd’s medical issues prompted his doctors to caution him against participating in contact sports. They felt it would lessen his chance of injuring his heart. In reality, he was too uncoordinated for sports, so he preferred not to be involved in school activities.

He usually sat at a lunch table with other disenfranchised classmates and rarely talked to anybody. He did, however, love cars. He excelled in auto shop, and despite his huge hands and seeming lack of coordination, Todd Linn turned out to be a pretty decent mechanic. After high school, he had gotten a job at the garage across Center Road near his parents’ pharmacy. Todd was also a bit of a savant regarding makes, models and years of almost every car he saw. He also knew who drove what car in Clarkwood.

His bedroom window lead directly out to the fire escape overlooking the alley. He used to joke that it was his perfect quick getaway when he didn’t feel like running into his parents. Todd had a separate front entrance to his apartment, but it was a few feet away from the pharmacy's front door, and invariably his mother would spot him and try to engage him in long, probing conversations, or his father would ask him to mind the store for an hour or so he could take a break.

Todd didn't like working at the pharmacy. While growing up, he struggled with several illnesses. He had been around the smells of medication and the sad visions of sick people and their families in doctors' offices and hospitals. He certainly didn't want to hang around the pharmacy and relive these unpleasantries.

As a teenager, Todd had been diagnosed with Marfan syndrome, a genetic disorder of the connective tissues that support the body's structures. Most people with this condition are unusually tall, with long, thin arms and legs, spider-like fingers, a sunken chest, and overly flexible joints. Their arm span is noticeably greater than their height. Many with Marfan syndrome can cross all fingers and toes, and bend their hands all the way back to where their fingers touch their forearm. Medical issues frequently occur like decreased muscle tone, cataracts and dislocation of the eye lenses, heart valve problems and learning disabilities. Research suggests that certain notable athletes, musicians, members of royalty and government, including Abraham Lincoln perhaps, have suffered from Marfan syndrome.

When he was fourteen years old, Todd had missed a good deal of school due to recurrent heart issues from a dissected aorta which ultimately led to him having an aortic valve replacement. Over the years, in addition to other medications, Todd's doctors prescribed "warfarin," an anticoagulant drug often incorrectly described as a blood thinner, to treat his condition.

Almost everyone, including Frank and Jeanette Linn, was at Mayor King Cotton's daughter's matrimonial reception by three o'clock in the afternoon so they wouldn't miss the wedding cake cutting. A live video of this ceremony was being projected on several gargantuan movie screens.

The supervisor of Streets and Sanitation was eyeing the grounds and figuring how many workers he would need to clean up after three thousand wedding guests. He also needed to arrange street sweeping for the several blocks along the route of the Labor Day Parade.

Todd Linn did not attend the momentous events of the day. He spent almost all morning and early afternoon lying on the couch in his apartment's small living room. While listening to the radio, he thumbed through a stack of auto magazines, making mental notes of the cars' appearances and features. Shortly after three o'clock, Todd switched off the radio because he thought he heard noises coming from the pharmacy which was closed for the holiday.

The noises moved to the alley in the rear of the building. Todd quickly went to the bedroom window that led to the fire escape, and peered out in time to see two young men, one carrying a large paper shopping bag, dashing down the alley towards the corner. They stopped short and reversed their direction, back across the alley and between two buildings a few doors down. Todd headed back to the living room and through the front windows saw the young men running across the street.

They sprinted to their cars, which were parked at the curb along the grassy part of the town square and sped off. Todd immediately recognized the two cars and their respective drivers. The 1995 aqua Nissan Sentra belonged to the tall, shadow-thin, dirty blonde-headed twenty-year-old Maurice "Maury" Clements. The badly dented mix-colored Ford Mustang convertible was owned by Maury's brother, equally tall, muscular, dark-haired nineteen-year-old Stephen "Soger" Clements. Stephen's father aptly nicknamed him Soger, an old nautical expression referring to a lazy shipmate who was always trying to avoid work. Maury and Soger suspected that their dad had been called that name in the Navy and had bestowed it on Stephen as a family heirloom. The brothers headed off to the wedding reception and illegally parked their cars in a loading zone just west of the train depot. They smiled at each other triumphantly as Maury stuffed the paper bag under the front passenger seat. As was the custom in Clarkwood, they left both cars unlocked, and then disappeared into the crowd of party-goers.

Todd's awareness suddenly focused on the wailing pharmacy burglar alarm, and he cautiously went down stairs. The pharmacy had been broken into through the rear door's ancient slide bolt, and the lock on the "controlled substances" cabinet had been easily snipped off with a bolt cutter. Missing was a variety of prescription drugs, including Valium®, Xanax®, Percocet®, Vicodin® and OxyContin®. No cash was taken, but dozens of candy bars and snacks were missing from the shelves – the same shelves Soger

Clements was asked to fill when he worked part-time as a stock boy at the Pharmacy the prior summer.

Todd Linn was somewhat doubtful that any law enforcement personnel would be at the Clarkwood Police station at mid-afternoon on Labor Day. The pharmacy's alarm system was not tied in with Clarkwood's Emergency Services, so the blaring security warning went as unnoticed as a car alarm set off by a careless parallel parker. He figured that all of the police officers would be eating wedding cake at the railroad station. Todd decided to walk down to the party and tell the police about the burglary himself. It took only a few minutes for local law enforcement to find and apprehend the brothers at the reception. In fact, it was Todd himself who spotted them weaving around the grounds looking dazed and impaired. With fingerprint and clothing fiber samples, the bag of stolen drugs in Maury's Sentra and the eyewitness testimony of Todd Linn, it looked to the police chief and Mayor Cotton like the trial would be a mere legal formality. However, as always, the suspects' father turned a blind eye to his boys' indiscretions and coughed up big bucks to hire a sharp legal team from Phoenix to represent Maury and Soger.

As the police continued to gather evidence to strengthen their case for the upcoming trial, Alex Everly Mann was called in to inspect the Linn's Pharmacy. Alex was an Arizona State Board of Pharmacy inspector, and because he lived in Prescott, his assignments were mostly in Northern Arizona. In this role, he was a state law enforcement officer who investigated pharmacy-related crimes, including fraud, robberies, and burglaries and he often served as an expert witness in court trials.

His initial impressions of the Linn Pharmacy were that it had been a burglary waiting to happen, and he was surprised that it hadn't happened sooner. Alex helped the Linns fill out and file the required DEA forms to document the loss of controlled substances. Over the next few days, he finished inspecting the drug store for security, recordkeeping, filing and storage of prescriptions and sales procedures.

Alex tried to consult with the Clarkwood Police Department. He wanted to share information that each had gathered so he could continue to develop his expert witness testimony. He also met with the Linns to review his recommendations for making their pharmacy more secure.

His "laundry list" included upgrades of front and rear doors and door locks, installation of an alarm system connected to Clarkwood's Emergency Services, computerization of customer and prescription records with off-site storage, and computer-generated prescription labels. Jeanette Linn was impressed by how thoroughly Alex had investigated and assessed the crime scene. Jeanette also saw Alex get tough when local law enforcement seemed less than enthusiastic about sharing information. After four days of the run-around, Alex went eyeball-to-eyeball with the Clarkwood Police detective sergeant, "You can cooperate with me voluntarily, or I can go way, way over your head. The guy I report to collaborates with the state attorney general on these matters," Alex said evenly.

The detective gritted his teeth and was about to explode on Alex, but he thought better of it. He was up for a promotion, and he had already been talked-to about controlling his temper and "playing nice" with others. He grudgingly shared with Alex what he knew about the pharmacy investigation. Despite the necessary arm twisting, the information helped Alex feel more confident about the upcoming legal proceedings.

When the trial of the Clements brothers began, the prosecution called only two witnesses besides the arresting officers: Todd Linn and Alex Mann. Throughout their testimonies, both received constant threatening glares and mouthed epithets from Maury and Soger. The defense attorney, as expected, refuted or dismissed all evidence presented by the prosecution. He tried to explain away the potentially damaging fingerprint and forensic evidence offered by the expert witness, Alex Mann by stating that the defendants frequented the Linn's drug store and that Soger Clements had been a stock boy there the previous summer. He asserted that half the town's citizens had spread their fingerprints and DNA all over the pharmacy. The defense attorney's final shot was to say in sotto voce, "It would seem that the cleaning efforts at the Linn Pharmacy were as ineffective as their security system."

He withdrew this remark after the prosecutor leapt to his feet to object. The young men's lawyer went on to contend that the rest of the case was flimsy and circumstantial. He stated that Todd Linn "had it in" for the defendants because when they were younger, the Clements boys had allegedly teased him about this height, skinny body and lack of sports prowess.

"Besides, even if Mr. Linn did see the boys near the pharmacy that day it was because they had stopped there hoping it was open so they could buy the mayor's daughter a wedding congratulations card. The boys didn't want to show up empty-handed – that's how they were raised, and that's how they are. Let's not convict these young men because they have proper manners." The defense counsel continued, "As far as seeing them running to their cars and driving hastily towards the reception, this only reinforces that the young men were anxious to get to the cake-cutting ceremony. Think about it – they ran toward the police, not away from them. It's already been established that both boys left their cars unlocked at the time the defendants were apprehended. Why would they do that if they were trying to hide something? Any one of the three thousand plus people at the reception could have easily tossed that bag of contraband under the seat of Maury's car."

The defense team decided that finding character witnesses for the Clements boys would be dicey, so they rested their case based on the reasonable doubt they hoped they had established. In spite of the defense attorney's impassioned closing remarks about their innocence, Maurice and Stephen Clements were convicted of second-degree burglary and illegal possession of controlled dangerous substances. Each received a sentence of three to five years in prison.

☼

After the February 17, 1997 Linn Pharmacy burglary trial and verdict, Alex and the Linn family said their good-byes. Alex would be advised of the Clements boys' sentences via an email from the prosecutor a few weeks later.

He had grown fond of the Linns. Alex appreciated their cooperation in the investigation and willingness to implement his suggestions to improve and secure the pharmacy. Jeanette and Frank Linn knew it was going to cost them a tidy sum of money, and would be a gamble in an extremely competitive market. Alex sincerely extended an invitation to them to call him anytime if they needed his help with pharmacy problems or issues related to the Clements trial. While she liked and trusted Alex, Jeanette Linn fervently hoped that her family's ill fortunes would turn around and that she wouldn't have to take Alex up on his offer.

As he drove west on Highway 89A from Clarkwood towards Prescott, Alex's mind was flooded with thoughts about the Linn investigation and subsequent trial. He was suddenly ravenous as his stomach untightened from the rigors of the trial and the Clements boys' intimidation. Alex decided to stop in the historic and colorful town of Jerome for a late lunch. He ate at a casual restaurant that, like most of the town's establishments, was allegedly haunted. In fact, Jerome boasts that it's the "Largest Ghost Town in America."

The food was tasty, and the friendly waitress wasn't spooky in the least, but Alex played into the legend and even bought an "I got the fright of my life in Jerome, AZ" key chain which was displayed prominently on a rack on the counter by the restaurant's cash register. He also stopped at a souvenir store and bought a biker T-shirt for his nephew that read, "I survived AZ 89A through Jerome, Arizona."

The previous summer, they had ridden their motor scooters on the same route to-and-from from Prescott through the road's legendary hairpin twists and turns. Now Alex could give his nephew his earned badge of honor.

After negotiating the winding thrill ride at dusk, Alex was finally off Mingus Mountain and on through Prescott Valley to Prescott. He looked forward to being home and catching up on the work he knew would be waiting for him. Still, at that moment, he couldn't imagine a future case as challenging as the one he had just completed.

3

Wednesday, July 26, 2000
Delmarva

Jeanette Linn was silent, yet visibly shaken for the remainder of her ride home from Neptune General Medical Center. She had just experienced the most grievous day of her life, and she didn't have Frank to help her make the emotionally-draining decisions she had just made. She had witnessed her son's death, donated his organs and sat through the autopsy, praying that the results would shed light on how Todd was killed.

Jeanette had no religious affiliations in Delmarva, but she wanted a clergy member present at Todd's funeral. At the doctor's suggestion, Jeanette decided to have a brief ceremony later that afternoon, conducted by the chaplain in the hospital's chapel. She and her friend, Virgie Meade-Worthington were the only other ones present to wish Todd a holy journey to a better place.

Sheriff Pickett hadn't hung around the hospital after Jeanette had signed the papers to take Todd off life support. He had no kind words for the grieving mother, nor did he have any intention of attending the ceremony. The sheriff finally reappeared at the hospital later that day to attend the autopsy review. As he was leaving, without saying a word, he brushed past Jeanette in the corridor and exited through a side entrance.

In accordance with Todd's wishes, on the following morning, the social worker at Neptune General contacted a local mortuary in Virginia Beach to pick-up Todd's body and have it cremated. Jeanette had asked that Todd's ashes be delivered to her in Delmarva.

Virgie pulled the El Dorado into Jeanette's crushed-rock driveway. She parked as close as possible to the front door, to save her friend unnecessary extra steps to her wheel chair. As soon as they entered the house, Virgie went into the kitchen to make them a pot of strong coffee. She then sat down on a bench at the breakfast nook while Jeanette searched for Alex's phone number through directory assistance. While she was waiting for the operator to retrieve the number, she murmured to Virgie, "How many men named Alex Everly Mann live in Prescott, let alone the state of Arizona?"

Alex was in his late fifties, no children, recently a widower, and very recently retired. He tried to stay as busy as possible to fill the emotional gaps left from the loss of his wife and career.

Having no trouble getting the phone number, she called Alex from her kitchen phone and after it rang eight times, Jeanette assumed his voicemail would take her message. Alex was delayed in answering the phone because he needed to find his reading glasses to see who was showing on his caller ID. Then it took Alex a few seconds to recognize the name.

He remembered the name but couldn't place the context. As a precaution, he lifted the receiver and spoke in a lower octave, in hopes it would throw off a caller with whom he didn't want to speak.

"Hello?"

"Is this Alex?"

"Umm – yes. Ahhh – I see your name on my phone ID. Mrs. Linn, how good to hear from you." He thought:

"At least I think it is."

"Mrs. Linn?" Jeanette inquired in surprise. "We used to be on a first-name basis, Alex! It's only been four years."

"Jeanette," Alex cried out. "My God, how are you? I'm sorry; I must confess I was napping. I guess I had a 'senior moment'."

"Don't worry about it. I have a few of them every day."

"How are Frank and Todd?" Alex asked as a social courtesy. He was shocked by her answer.

"They're dead. They're both dead." Jeanette said almost mechanically. "Frank died in '98. His bad heart, you know."

"I am so sorry, Jeanette. I lost my Betty to cancer two years ago." Then, in a rapid flurry of queries, Alex asked, "What happened to Todd? You say *he's* passed away too? When? Was it the Marfan? Was it his heart? Was he taking his warfarin?"

Jeanette was silent for a few seconds; as if she were collecting her thoughts and trying to control her emotions. "Todd died a few hours ago in the hospital; I told them it was okay to let him die. I feel like I let him down. Like I gave up on him."

Alex cut in. "Jeanette, don't blame yourself. Was he sick? Was he in an accident? How long was he on life support?" He caught himself. "I'm truly sorry I'm bombarding you with questions like an investigator, it's just that…"

Jeanette cut in. "You're doing exactly what I hoped you would do. Alex, I need an investigator. I want to know how Todd died. I think he was murdered!"

Alex seemed to brush right over Jeanette's statement. "What hospital was he in? Green Valley Medical Center?" I knew some people there before I retired. I used to inspect their pharmacy."

"It wasn't Green Valley, Alex; we moved from Clarkwood shortly after Frank died. We – I live on the East Coast now in a town named Delmarva. It's between Baltimore and Norfolk, Virginia," Jeanette interjected. "Todd died out here at Neptune General."

Although Alex had ventured through most areas of the United States and several foreign countries, he had no real contacts on the Eastern seaboard. Quickly he seized the importance of what Jeanette had said.

"Why are you sure Todd was murdered? Is that what the autopsy concluded? What happened? Was he assaulted? Who do you think murdered him?"

Jeanette shot back, "I didn't say I was sure he was murdered. I said I *think* he was murdered. They say Todd died from a brain hemorrhage, but I don't know what really happened. That's the point. I want to be convinced, I want the facts. Todd told me that he had been jumped by three guys on the docks, and one of them hit him over the head with a tire iron. I told this to our county sheriff, George Pickett, but he says that Todd fell down the steps at Monty Tipsword's trailer, and hit his head on the ground. Sheriff Pickett says that he has a witness that will corroborate this. Todd didn't look like he had been hit with a tire iron, but I don't know why he would lie to me?"

Alex started to speak, but Jeanette talked over him. "According to our sheriff, 'It was a terrible accident and what's done is done – case closed.' Anyway, as I said before, I want the truth. I really think Todd was murdered one way or another." She sighed, "Look Alex, I want to be straight with you. I'm dying too. I've got lung cancer that's spreading and my diabetes has gotten so bad that they took my left leg below the knee. I don't have much to live for, especially now, but I will spend my last dollar and my last breath getting justice for Todd."

Alex was stunned and saddened by Jeanette Linn's predicament. "Oh Jeanette – I don't know what to say – I can't imagine what you're going through. Please tell me what I can do, how I can help?"

Jeanette gratefully acknowledged Alex's offer of assistance. "I know this is asking a lot. You told me when we said goodbye after the Clements trial that I could call you anytime I needed your help. I hope the offer hasn't expired after four years."

"Of course the offer still stands!" said Alex in a reassuring tone. "Whatever I can do, Jeanette."

"I don't even know if you are available, but...Alex, I need you to come out here and find out what really happened to my son. I trust you, and you're a person who has known my family. I have always admired how you handled yourself while you were investigating our pharmacy burglary in Clarkwood. We felt like you honestly cared about us. I also like that you aren't tied in with any of our town politics. Sheriff Pickett's so-called law enforcement investigation was delayed several days because they had wrong information about what day, what place and what witnesses truly saw. When I talked to him at the hospital this morning, the sheriff practically told me that the case was closed. But it's not closed, Alex. Seems like he and his deputies don't really want to know what actually happened. Will you help me figure things out?"

"I don't know what I can really do Jeanette, but I am available. Don't worry about paying me a fee. All I ask for are the usual travel and expenses, and oh – I'm probably going to need some assistance. I know the perfect person, a talented former student and sometimes colleague named Winnie who owes me one or two favors. She has a truly caring heart and fierce determination."

"That's very nice of you and your associate but fortunately; money problems are the one thing I *don't* have right now."

After the investigation and the Clements trial, the Linns did all of the pharmacy-related things that Alex had told them to do. Their drug store was running more efficiently, had much-improved security, and in all, business was good. The following year Frank took sick and Jeanette had trouble running things at the pharmacy while also taking care of him. It was not only difficult, but quite expensive to find a pharmacist willing to travel to a rural area to work. Todd wanted no part of working there. When Frank died in 1998, Jeanette's heart wasn't in the business anymore, and she no longer wanted to own the pharmacy. A new "Prescriptions 'n' Things" had just opened in the nearby town of Wooldale, and that started to seriously cut into their business.

Jeanette talked to Todd about the fact that he had been out of work since he was laid-off at the garage more than four months before. They both knew that job opportunities had dried-up in Clarkwood. Jeanette explained that it was less about her needing extra money and more about him needing to work for his own self-esteem. While he was unemployed, Todd would mope around and sometimes not leave his apartment for several days at a time. They agreed that he needed to be kept busy, or he and Jeanette would drive each other crazy.

A few weeks later, Todd bumped into a former high school classmate who was in town visiting his family. He told Todd he was crewing on a sixty-five-foot commercial fishing boat that was docked in the Atlantic coastal town of Delmarva. He said that they needed big guys like Todd to help haul in fish nets and transfer the catch to the insulated stainless steel ice tanks.

Todd asked his friend, "I won't have to climb masts, will I? I'm not good with heights."

His friend started laughing and said, "Toddler, relax, the boat is mostly powered by the engines. We do use the sails on nice days, but nobody has to climb to the crow's nest." In truth, Jeanette found out later that if the fishing boat had sailed up and ran into an unexpected storm, one or more of the crew might very well have to climb up to untangle a line or sail. He may have over-romanticized the job and the town, and even though it wasn't car mechanics, Todd was clearly interested.

A few months, later Jeanette was contacted by a developer who wanted to do an extensive downtown renewal. The Linn’s pharmacy wasn’t in his plans, but it was smack-dab in the middle of everything; prime real estate. She sold the building to the developer for a generous profit. Along with the money Jeanette made selling their prescription files, and with Frank’s life insurance and military pension, she was financially able to consider the option of Todd and her moving away from the painful memories of Clarkwood.

Todd’s finding that job as a coastal fishing boat crew member was a key reason why they moved from Arizona to Delmarva. Jeanette’s medical conditions had worsened, and she thought about their relatives that lived nearby on the east coast. When she told them that they were moving to Delmarva they had seemed enthusiastic and supportive. It would have been extremely difficult for Todd to care for Jeanette by himself, and she had hoped that they could reach out to their relatives if they needed to.

It had taken about three months for Todd and Jeanette to complete the sale of their prescription files and property before moving to Delmarva. During that time, a realtor friend of Jeanette’s in Clarkwood had recommended that they hire a real estate agent, one of her former colleagues, who had transferred to the company’s branch office in Challenger County. She had started house shopping for the Linns a few weeks before they moved, and once they had arrived in town, she had lined up a half a dozen houses for Todd and Jeanette to look at. They especially liked two of the homes but decided on the gray two-story Cape Cod. It was located right in Delmarva, very near Challenger Harbor. In the meantime, they stayed at Granny Pickett's Bed & Breakfast, the only game in town. They were able to close on the house in thirty days and moved in shortly thereafter.

Bad luck began for the Linns when Todd's high school friend, the only shipmate he knew on-board, abandoned the fishing boat after a few days and was never in contact with Todd again. Next, despite her efforts to keep in touch with their local relatives, Jeanette hadn't received a return phone call, letter, or even an email from any of them since a month after they moved to town, two years prior. So distant was their relationship with one another that Jeanette hadn't even called them about coming to the hospital for Todd's funeral service. She doubted that they would have come anyway.

Todd started to get settled into his new job as a hauler and loader on a mid-sized, twin-masted commercial fishing boat aptly named, "The Challenger," in honor of the county and the harbor. Todd wasn't a morning person and liked to sleep as late as possible. He was pleased with his short travel time to work, and though he wasn't known for his witty comments, he would indelicately tell people, particularly when he drank a lot of beer that he lived so close to the boat that he could start peeing in his bathroom toilet at home and finish in the harbor's restroom without dribbling a single drop along the way. The joke received little more than a half-smiling, eye-rolling grunt from those who heard it.

Even after she had bought the new house and vehicles, Jeanette was sitting on a rather substantial nest egg. She decided to invest her money locally. She had hoped it would make life easier in Delmarva for Todd and her. She soon discovered what it meant to be an *away* in that town.

Jeanette had made several unsuccessful attempts to get involved with business and community affairs. While exploring her options, she found out that her poor health was almost as dismal as the monetary state of the town's only financial institution, a privately-held loan company. It was the source of cash overwhelmingly used by Delmarva's businesses and citizens, particularly commercial fishermen and their families. Few people had any savings at all, and for those who did, the security and availability of their money were in serious doubt. These were tough economic times in Delmarva. Many customers defaulted on their loans. The lending company's owners ended up running out of cash to make any new loans, and called back all but a few existing loans. Jeanette sat down with the owners of the loan company to "make them an offer they couldn't refuse." She asked to buy their near-bankrupt financial institution, thereby saving the town's citizens and businesses their capital lifelines. She wanted to be an *away* who gained some respect and admiration in Delmarva. She also figured that she would have a favor to call in and strings to pull if she ever needed to do so.

While her offer was tempting, the town's "powers that be," which included Sheriff Pickett, flatly refused to approve it and cited the fact that a one-owner business, and in particular a financial institution, would give too much power to a single *away*. The sheriff wanted to maintain almost complete authority. Even the mayor cleared most things first with Challenger County's top lawman.

Jeanette was disappointed, but not surprised, with the decision. As a smart business woman, she immediately scrambled to come up with a Plan B.

Fortunately, six weeks later she was delighted when the town's loan company folded and those same powers that be practically begged her to open her own business. In a few weeks, Jeanette had the bankrupt loan office spruced up, and had debuted her new and improved loan company, aptly named Float-A-Check. While the interest rates were high, they were legal, negotiable and available.

For the most part, Todd did not ease into the Demarvan culture, such as it was. He sometimes had angry words and shoving matches with crew mates who felt Todd was not only an *away,* but a lazy one at that. In truth, it wasn't that he was unambitious or trying to avoid work, it was that the effects of the Marfan syndrome and chronic pain genuinely slowed him down. Lately, he had been having trouble grasping the lines because his joints were too limber. Another problem was that since Frank died, Jeanette's medical condition had gotten worse, and Todd had gained an enormous amount of weight – almost two hundred pounds. This made it much more difficult for him to get around and for his doctor to regulate his medication, especially his warfarin.

Before they ended their phone call, Alex inserted a caveat to his offer of assistance. "Jeanette, one more thing. I need to tell you honestly that I can't guarantee you that my investigation will come up with the answers you're looking for. I have to follow the clues where they lead me. For instance, if you think someone named Monty Tipsword murdered Todd at a party and I find out that he didn't, I don't want it to seem like I turned against you."

"I do understand, Alex. I talked to Todd that Saturday morning when he came home from Monty's party. He told me three guys had beaten him up, and he would get even with them. But, he died a few days later, and I think Monty Tipsword had something to do with it. If Todd didn't tell me the truth about being hit with a tire iron, then I wonder if he was truthful about three guys being there. This is where I'd like you to concentrate your efforts – finding out if there were three people present, and if so, who they are and if they played a role in Todd's death."

Alex knew there were many layers of evidence that needed to be excavated. He told Jeanette, "As soon as I figure out where Delmarva is, I'll fly out to you and we'll have a chance to talk more.

"Sure," she replied, "for now, I have time. Who knows for how long? I want to stay alive long enough to see that the law punishes Monty Tipsword or whoever killed my son."

Alex was deeply moved by Jeanette's hardships. It seemed like the same black clouds that plagued her and Todd in Clarkwood had followed them to Delmarva and picked up a few "friends" along the way.

4

Tuesday, June 13, 2000
Prescott, Arizona

Alex had pushed the memories of the Clements boys and their trial out of his mind, but more than three years later he received an unexpected email from Mayor Bart "King" Cotton of Clarkwood, Arizona.

"Good day, Inspector Mann – first off, I am proud to tell you that I am a grandfather of a chubby-cheeked little tyke. Buffy and Troy named him Bart, after yours truly. Naturally we call him 'The Little Prince.' I like to joke that he's the heir to the King Cotton throne.

I also wanted to let you know that the Clements boys were just released after serving their time in our fair prison. Those boys are what you call downright 'unpredictable.' I have the Linns' email address, and I'll pass the warning along to them. Watch your back and take good care."

Alex remembered the glowering and mumbled threats directed at him and the Linns by Maury and Soger Clements during their burglary trial. He emailed Mayor Cotton back and congratulated him on his grandson. He also thanked him for the heads-up and assured the mayor that he'd keep his eyes open and his guard up. Alex began to feel that the distance between Prescott and Clarkwood had just become too close for comfort.

5

Wednesday, July 19, 2000
Delmarva

Less than a month after Mayor Cotton's email to Alex, the "unpredictableness" of the Clements brothers was clearly demonstrated. Around midnight, a sheriff's deputy was patrolling the quiet streets of Delmarva. About a quarter of a mile from Jeanette Linn's house, the deputy spotted a car with an Arizona license plate idling on the road's shoulder. He pulled in behind the other car and activated the squad car's flashing lights.

The deputy walked up to the vehicle and shined his flashlight at the driver's window. Maury Clements peered out at him, and he and Soger scrunched down in their seats as if to avoid detection. The deputy sheriff was momentarily humored by the boys' antics, but he rapped vigorously with his flashlight on the front windshield.

"Please step out of the car, boys."

"What's the problem, Officer?" asked Soger.

"That's my question to you, and let's not play games. You're from out of state, you're pulled over on the shoulder in the middle of nowhere at twelve-thirty in the morning, and you tried to avoid me by crawling on the floor of your car."

The Clements boys looked blankly at the deputy, then Maury spoke up, "I know this looks bad, sir, but I can explain. See, we're from Clarkwood,

Arizona, and we're old neighbors of the Linn family. It was a shame that they moved so far away, and Soger and I started thinking that it would be cool to take a road trip and visit our old neighbors. And heck, it took a lot longer to get here than we thought. We got lost a few times, and the next thing we know we're on a dark road at midnight – really lost! When you came along we were just about to look at the map for the tenth time. We were a little startled when you shined that flashlight in our eyes, and, well, I'm not ashamed to admit, a little scared too. That's why we slunk down the way we did." Soger nodded his head vigorously in agreement.

The deputy slowly shook his head and sighed disbelievingly. While the boys stood by their car with their hands on the hood, he checked their driver's licenses and Arizona plates. He wanted to verify their story, but did not want to call the Linn house so late and disturb or frighten the ailing Jeanette and rile up Todd. The deputy again shone his flashlight in their faces and asked them several more questions.

"Were the Linns expecting you? Have you been in touch with Todd or Jeanette? Were you going to stay with them tonight? Did you come all the way from Northern Arizona just to visit the Linns?"

To all of these questions, Maury and Soger took turns answering with, "Not exactly."

No red flags appeared on their background checks. The Clements brothers were first-time offenders, and after serving their sentences, their criminal records were expunged. Given that the boys had no "wants or warrants," the deputy's hands were tied in terms of making an arrest. He noted their names and reluctantly released them. He surely did not want the Clements boys in town.

The deputy warned them to clear out, and if he saw them again, they would be arrested for suspicious behavior. He then escorted the boys out of town and watched them drive away. The deputy strongly suspected that the Clements brothers had not come to Delmarva to embrace the Linns. He felt that he had let them slip through his fingers, but was powerless to stop them. He wondered, with some ambivalence if he would cross paths with them again.

6

Friday, July 21, 2000
Delmarva

Since moving to Delmarva, Todd mostly kept to himself after work, but he did occasionally date some of the young ladies in town. He got mixed reviews from the women with whom he socialized. One or two said he was nice and polite while others said he was aggressive when he drank beer. One said he was "kinda creepy" after she told him she wasn't interested in a second date with him. He stalked her for about a week; driving by her house at all hours of the night.

His current girlfriend was named Juanda Tipsword. Her nickname was "Tipsy" because of her last name, or perhaps because she liked to drink a bit and was a tad flighty. She seemed genuinely fond of Todd and she worried about him getting into fights; one the main forms of recreation for young males in Delmarva. Juanda tried to make sure that he took his warfarin and his other medications. In fact, Todd had put her in charge of his meds. She was much better than he was at remembering things like that. At first, he complained a lot when she gave him his medications, but he grew to enjoy the attention and allowed himself to trust Juanda.

Todd Linn liked to drink beer, and he liked being around other people, but only after he had downed a six-pack. Because he rarely got invited, Todd often crashed parties which sprang up sometimes on weekdays, but usually on Saturday nights. The hosts usually let Todd come in because he always brought a keg of "imported" (out-of-state) beer with him. They would drink his beer but showed him little in the way of friendship or acceptance. The long periods of time that Todd had been ill and missed school not only hindered his academic progress, but also his social skills. Todd's attempts at even starting or continuing a conversation were generally awkward at best.

Since more than doubling his weight over the past two or three years, Todd's grossly expanded appearance was a bit of a spectacle in Delmarva and his six feet eight inch, three hundred and fifty pound body seemed more massive with each step he took towards you. His doctor wasn't sure what caused the extreme weight gain, and the results of further medical tests were also inconclusive. It may have been related to the Marfan, or Todd's various medications, or as some suggested, his depression about losing his father, worrying about his mother's failing health and moving to a town where he had few friends and a job he hated. The harder Todd tried to assimilate into the Demarvan community, the more he was disliked by the locals.

There was a party at Monty Tipsword's mobile home on the Friday night of July 21, 2000, for no special reason other than there hadn't been a party since around the Fourth of July. Monty's trailer was smallish, in a state of disrepair, and smelled considerably of beer, fish and stale tobacco smoke. This ambiance seemed to draw in the area residents, particularly the men. Monty and Todd crewed on the "Challenger" together and had a barely bearable relationship. Juanda Tipsword also crewed with them and happened to be Monty's first cousin. She and her mother lived in a larger trailer across the dirt road from Monty's. Juanda tried hard not to get caught up in taking sides when Monty and Todd quarreled.

Monty came from a long line of fishermen, and his grandfather, who was warmly referred to as the "Godfather," valiantly fought off thugs and would-be competitors for control of Delmarva's tiny fishing industry.

His father became the new Godfather several years later, and relied on his kin to keep the business up and running. Nobody ever accused Monty of being lazy. He worked a long, physically demanding shift each day crewing on the Challenger. Many said his weaknesses were that he lacked the two previous Godfathers' leadership skills and overall drive needed to take over the business one day." Monty preferred to be known as *the* party host in Delmarva. His father, of course, was inwardly disappointed with his son's lack of ambition but maintained a brave face in the presence of the other fishermen.

Todd had gotten wind of Monty's party first hand as he dropped off Juanda after driving her home from work. It was about six-thirty, and a small stream of party guests were coming and going from Monty's trailer. The loudness of the music and animated voices increased proportionally with the amount of beer that was consumed. A few revelers were sitting outside on the empty kegs from this and past parties, and either side of the mobile home was strewn with beer cans and bottles overflowing from the trash cans. There were so many used beer glasses and mugs in the sink that Monty had to “clean” each one as needed by swirling bar grade whiskey around inside.

Todd Linn mentioned to Juanda that he was thinking about them going over to Monty’s for a while. She shook her head purposefully and reminded Todd that he and Monty had quarreled on the fishing boat Wednesday, and also pointed out the fact that they had not been invited.

“Look Juanda,” said Todd. “You were there; you saw Monty stand by and watch while the net nearly ripped my hand off. Anyway, we didn’t have any fight, just yelling.”

Todd made sure to call her Juanda and not Tipsy, especially when he was trying to plead his case to her about some contentious issue they were battling about. Neither of them liked their nicknames. Todd felt that “Toddler” connoted an oversized, stumbling person with limited intelligence, while Juanda believed that “Tipsy” referred to a perpetual drunk with loose morals.

“Todd, you know we’d have lost half the catch if my cousin had let go of the net to help you.”

Todd continued, “And since when do we need an invitation to his parties. We’re kin and neighbors for God’s sake.”

“No,” Juanda raised her voice, “*I’m* his kin and neighbor. Not *us*.”

Todd recoiled at her remark and said, “Well I’m going over there, and I’d like it if you came too, but I’m going either way.”

“Fine,” Juanda replied, “You go. I’m staying here.” She glared at Todd, and then her face softened and showed concern. “Really though, be careful Todd.

When you drink too much you start feeling poorly, and you get angry too. I don't want you fighting with Monty."

Todd nodded at Juanda and headed to his truck, a 1998 Chevrolet Suburban which had been advertised at the time as "the largest and most powerful sports utility vehicle on the planet." To raise their spirits after months of heartache with the death of Frank Linn and the decline of Linn Pharmacy, Jeanette had treated Todd to the truck and bought herself her dream car, a brand new Cadillac Eldorado, shortly before they had moved to Delmarva.

Before going to Monty's party, Todd drove to Swigs Liquors, had a quick chat with the owner, Swigs Buser. His mother was a Pickett who married a wealthy *away*, but who kept the liquor store in her name to avoid opposition from the people in town about *away* business ownership. The senior Swigs was well-liked and was famous for making a twelve-pack of beer a baker's dozen by adding a can. He died with his shop apron on at age fifty-seven while unloading a case of lite beer and his son took over the store as soon as he turned twenty-one.

Swigs treated Todd as a special customer because of the volume of beer he bought, and because Jeanette Linn had made Swigs a business loan through her newly acquired private loan company. Todd left Swigs Liquors with a chilled keg of beer brewed in Milwaukee, Wisconsin. Milwaukee was far enough away from Delmarva for Todd to call it imported beer.

When Todd returned to Monty's trailer, the foot traffic to and from the party was slow, but steady. Todd held up the keg over his head and nodded to Monty as he climbed the three steps to the front door of the trailer. He crouched down low to fit his towering frame through the opening, and remained crouched while he was in the trailer. Monty nodded back and showed Todd where to put the keg in the tiny galley kitchen. As he looked around, Todd recognized all but one of the guests, and that guy happened to look a lot like Monty. He wondered if he was an out-of-town relative of the Tipswords.

An easy census search would have confirmed that there was an abundance of Tipswords in a two hundred mile radius of Challenger County. As Todd looked closer at the mystery *away*, he realized that even by Delmarva standards, this guy seemed unsavory and shifty. “Shifty” was a term Todd’s mother used to describe certain customers that came into the pharmacy looking to buy narcotics with forged prescriptions. Judging from his beat-up hands and sea-legs walk, Todd figured he was a fisherman on a coastal boat that probably docked somewhere further north of Delmarva.

The mystery *away* latched onto Todd and tried to help him tap into a keg. Todd asked too harshly, “Does it look like I need help?”

“No, I’m betting you don’t. It looks like you could handle two kegs at once at your size.”

From the right side of the kitchen counter, Todd picked up a large beer stein with a soggy cigarette butt floating near the bottom. He poured the contents into the sink, and without rinsing it, he filled the stein with his imported beer.

Sensing that the mystery *away* was a bit put-off by his attitude, Todd held up the beer stein and told him, “I’ll like you better after I’ve had a few more of these.” Somewhat placated, the stranger moved on to the small living room and started flirting with some of the local women by offering them Todd's premium beer.

Todd had been particularly chatty during the party and had bent the ears of several guests. He mostly talked about his former job as a car mechanic in Clarkwood, and bragged about the fact that his mother was the proud owner of a new loan company in town. Bored guests managed to escape Todd's drunken ramblings by drifting away slowly to other conversations. Some even left the trailer.

Suddenly secretive, Todd didn't want to reveal any details of why Juanda wasn't at the party. Earlier in the evening, when a few of Todd's acquaintances asked about her, he almost inaudibly mumbled any excuse he could think of at the moment. As the evening went on, and the kegs were emptying, Todd's answers became wilder: Juanda had gotten lost and couldn't find Monty's trailer; Juanda had been in an accident and was in a full plaster body cast; Juanda was mud wrestling against Laila Ali, and so forth.

The party began to wind down about ten-thirty and Monty was looking to clear out the guests so he could go to sleep. He had already decided that he wouldn't waste a minute cleaning up any cans, bottles or assorted garbage from the party until the next morning. It would all be there waiting for him.

Todd was obviously not "getting" that the party was over, and all of the guests, save one, had left. The mystery *away* that Todd had been short with a few hours ago remained immobile on the sofa. Monty didn't like being ignored, and became more forceful in expressing his request.

The mystery *away* bolted up when Monty yelled, "Clear out – bar's closed!"

"Just one final leak for the road," said the mystery *away* and headed into the small bathroom.

Todd was still not making any effort to leave, and Monty became angry when he watched Todd gulp down a half-empty bottle of warm beer, then doze off a few seconds later on one of the kitchen chairs. Monty strode over and clapped his hands loudly in front of Todd's face. "Hey Toddlin' Toddler. Party's over, bar's closed. Tipsy probably don't want to see you in this shape. Go sleep it off somewhere, but not here!"

Todd made no response, so Monty tried to pull him up from the chair. Todd pushed Monty's hands off his enormous shoulders, and yelled, "Keep your paws off me, Monty. I don't want to stay here anyway. There's no more beer, and this place stinks like cigarettes and fish. I hate cigarettes and fish."

Monty held back his anger as he took hold of Todd's left elbow and started to point him in the direction of the door. Todd pulled his arm away from Monty and shouted, "Lay off, I'm leaving!"

Todd stumbled clumsily to the trailer's open door and banged his head on the lintel as he started to exit. He spun around, knocked over an end table at the side of the sofa, shuffled his feet backward, and then bumped into the window air conditioner unit. Todd pitched forward and took long, shaky strides towards the door again. This time he ducked his head, but pitched forward, stumbled down the three trailer steps, and landed face down in a pile of wood chips a few feet from the steps.

The mystery *away* joined Monty at the doorway. They peered down at Todd who was motionless and appeared to be unconscious. Neither could be sure if Todd's current state was from his excessive alcohol consumption or from his fall down the steps.

Monty walked down from the trailer and stood over Todd's body. He noticed that Todd had dropped his truck keys, so he snatched them up, took a fistful of cash from the wallet in Todd's back pants pocket, then he and his remaining party guest raced all over Delmarva in Todd's truck, honking and yelling out of the windows as they indulged in the time-honored Demarvan tradition called the "Tanked-up Victory Drive." The noises pierced through the quiet of the sleeping neighborhoods, but most of the residents paid little attention to the disturbance. Their only concern was finding out who out-drank who – but that would have to wait until morning.

7

Wednesday, July 26, 2000
Prescott

The day after his lengthy phone conversation with Jeanette on the day of Todd's death, Alex cleared his somewhat light schedule and arranged to meet with her in Delmarva that Friday. His now-deceased wife, Betty used to handle all of the travel arrangements for Alex's free-lance jobs. Since her death, he employed Betty's cousin, Freda who was skilled at booking him a center seat, at the back of the plane, two rows from the restrooms. Luckily, he was almost always able to switch to a better seat at the gate. Betty was extremely close to Freda and had gotten her started in the travel agent business.

Alex thought:

"So, this one's for you, Betts."

He asked Freda if she had any favors from the airlines to call in. Despite poor past performance, she surprisingly got him a reasonably-priced aisle seat on a plane that departed from Phoenix at ten o'clock the following morning. Alex took an early-morning two-hour shuttle ride from Prescott to Phoenix Sky Harbor International Airport (PHX). Freda also booked his accommodations in Challenger County for the first night. Alex packed one suitcase and made sure he had several lenses in his camera case. Photography was not only a hobby and a passion for him, but also an invaluable tool during investigations.

8

Thursday, July 27 & Friday, July 28, 2000
Delmarva

Jeanette Linn had reassured Alex that she was financially solvent, which allowed Alex to book non-stop flights and accommodations at decent motels. Initially, Jeanette had offered Alex the use of Todd's truck while he was investigating for her, but Alex had pointed out that the vehicle may be held as evidence. There was no mention of Jeanette loaning him her Eldorado. Alex had no idea how long his investigation would last or how many miles he would drive pursuing witnesses and obtaining evidence. Freda recommended that he rent cars as needed from a nationwide agency with whom she did business that could give him the best rates.

Alex's flight departed on schedule from PHX and arrived at Baltimore-Washington International (BWI) five hours later. He waited only a few minutes to board the shuttle to the rental car agency where Freda had made a reservation in Alex's name. He had hoped for a larger, less obtrusive vehicle, but she had gotten him a low weekly rental rate on a 1998 red Toyota Celica convertible. It was eye-catching and stylish; just the things Alex was not looking for in an investigator's car. He was able to convince the car rental dealer to make him the same deal on a white 1997 Mercury Sable wagon. By the time he finished signing the paperwork, it was nearly six o'clock in the evening.

Leaving BWI, Alex took I-95 South to Annapolis, Maryland, drove south over the Chesapeake Bay Bridge, and finally arrived in the Challenger County area about three hours later.

Alex had accommodations at the Safe Travels Inn about twenty minutes outside of Delmarva. He had eaten a sandwich at the airport around ten o'clock that morning but hadn't had anything since. The motel's coffee shop had closed at eight o'clock, and they did not offer room service. There were vending machines on both floors, but they only sold cans of soda. There was a 24-hour pancake restaurant almost within walking distance of the motel, but Alex was too tired to go out again. The long day had gotten the better of him. With his shoes still on, Alex flopped on the non-smoking room's king-size bed, and channel surfed through the local television stations for about fifteen minutes.

He could have slept like that all night, but Betty had been a stickler about preparing for bed. Alex slipped off his shoes and socks, hung his clothes over the back of the chair, ran the toothbrush over his teeth, and slept in his underwear.

He slept through two seven o'clock morning wake up calls. Finally, a little after seven-thirty, he grudgingly sat up in bed, took a few deep yoga breaths and then quickly showered and dressed. Just after he retired from his pharmacy inspector job, friends had suggested that Alex take up yoga for exercise and relaxation. The breathing exercises were what he enjoyed and benefitted most from. To Alex, it seemed odd at first when his yoga teacher read an adage from a dog-eared page of the "Little Zen Calendar" which read:

"Knowledge is learning something every day.
Wisdom is letting go of something every day."

This yoga stuff was new to him. Alex knew he didn't grasp every nuance of spiritual meaning from what she had said, but he was intrigued by the notion. His career as a pharmacist and investigator steered him to be rational and clinical in his thinking and dealings with others. Alex did, however, acknowledge that mental breakthroughs, or what his teacher had called "satoris," sometimes occurred when he stopped pressing, and just let them come to him.

Making a mental note to find a room closer to Delmarva, Alex checked-out of his motel. He was due at Jeanette Linn's house at nine-fifteen that morning. In Delmarva, everyone picked up their mail at the post office, so there were no street addresses. Instead, Alex had to rely on complicated turn-by-turn directions and descriptions from Jeanette to find the house.

He arrived exactly on time and was immediately impressed with her beautiful if somewhat modest two-story Cape Cod home. Like many houses in the area, it was painted a flat gray, and there were four steps leading up to the white-trimmed front porch. Todd had built a ramp on the right side of the steps to accommodate his mother's wheel chair. The second floor had two dormer windows and the roof held a chimney exactly in the center of the peak.

Alex was shocked at Jeanette's appearance when she came to the front door to greet him. It had been four years since he had last seen her. Illness and grief had aged and weakened her considerably. They exchanged a sincere embrace, and Alex took a step back and placed his hands on Jeanette's shoulders. "Jeanette, it's wonderful to see you again. You look…"

Jeanette stopped Alex from finishing his comment by putting her index finger over her lips. He realized that she was beyond false flattery or polite banter.

"Alex, you're a godsend. Once again you've come to my rescue."

He wanted to tell her that she needed to have realistic expectations about his success in solving the case. Then he tried to imagine her grief. Alex decided to talk to Jeanette about that later.

She grimaced as she slowly moved about using crutches.

"Are you able to wear a prosthesis?" Alex asked as he eyed her left leg.

"No – too damned painful, and what's the use anyway. I can hardly get around with it, or without it," Jeanette said. There was no self-pity in her voice. With a flourish of her right hand, she motioned for Alex to take a tour of her home. Despite its seashore location, Jeanette had the living room coffee table, fireplace mantel and dining room hutches crowded with knickknacks and mementos from her life in Arizona.

It was obvious that she cared about how the house looked and was pleased that Todd hadn't seemed to mind helping with landscaping and simple maintenance chores when he wasn't out crewing on the local fishing boat.

They walked slowly into the kitchen. Jeanette's friend, Virgie was making coffee. She had been staying with Jeanette to help out with chores since Todd's death. Alex introduced himself as he reached out his hand to Virgie. She had a reassuring smile, a pleasant face and long gray-streaked brown hair pulled back in a ponytail. She started to leave the room after serving coffee, but Jeanette wanted her to stay. Jeanette glanced questioningly at Alex, who nodded his approval. Virgie remained silent throughout the meeting. They sat at a large free-form shaped kitchen table made of highly polished coastal driftwood.

Alex wanted Jeanette to give him a better picture of what had happened on the Saturday and Sunday after Monty Tipsword's party. "Jeanette, what time did he come home Friday night? Or was it Saturday morning?"

"I don't know. I didn't see him until about noon on Saturday. He came hobbling downstairs and said that his left leg wouldn't do what he wanted it to do. He didn't know why, but he said that three guys out on the docks had jumped him from behind and hit him in the head with a tire iron. I said that he'd better even the score if he knew who they were. Maybe I shouldn't have said that, but Todd was picked-on a lot by the other fishermen because of his appearance and because we're from *away*. I was tired of it. He looked like he was in so much pain and I told him that if his leg wasn't better by Monday that he needed to go to the clinic."

"Did Todd agree to that?"

"Yes he did. Probably more for me than for himself.

What did he do next?"

"He fried a turkey for me, but he had a hard time. If we had a turkey in the fridge, then it wasn't necessary to cook for the rest of the week."

"Why did he have a hard time?"

"Because he was hobbling and he had a bad headache that he said was from a hangover."

"Did he take anything for the headache?"

"A bunch of ibuprofen. I also reminded him not to forget his warfarin because he didn't want to get a blood clot from getting hit in the head. I watched him struggle to get back up to his room, and the next time I saw him was later Saturday afternoon."

"How did he seem then?"

"No better – maybe worse. I had been taking a nap and didn't feel like getting up, so he came to my room. He offered to make me something to eat, but I told him I wasn't hungry. He went ahead and ate a turkey sandwich and took some more ibuprofen. Then he went back upstairs. I never saw my son alive again."

9

Sunday, July 23, 2000
Jeanette Linn's House & Neptune General Hospital
&
Monday, July 24 - Wednesday July 26, 2000
Neptune General Medical Center

"Challenger County 911. May I have your location?"

"Jeanette Linn's house," Todd Linn responded.

"What is your emergency?"

"My left leg won't move."

"What is your name, sir?"

"Todd, Todd Linn.

"Do you know why your leg won't move?"

"I was beaten over the head."

"Stay on the phone with me; we have an ambulance on the way."

The time of the call was two twenty-five on Sunday morning. Considering the early hour and the close proximity of the Delmarva Medical Clinic to Jeanette Linn's house, the EMTs elected not to use the red lights and siren. Jeanette was sleeping in the back bedroom on the first floor. She was heavily medicated and had oxygen running, so she was not awakened by the sound and commotion in her living room.

Lead EMT, Hillary Hedgpeth held open the front door and motioned for her male associate to enter the home.

They discovered Todd Linn, dressed only in a pair of blue shorts, struggling unsuccessfully to rise from the couch. She told him to try to relax and to please stay seated where he was. His great weight was going to make it difficult for just two people to get him into the ambulance. Hillary decided to conduct her assessment of Todd on his living room couch. She called out observations and readings to her EMT associate, who recorded them in a medical log. While she was performing Todd's assessment, Hillary heard the radio message dispatching a sheriff's officer to investigate a reported assault. She was relieved to know that she would have the additional manpower needed to help transfer Todd to the ambulance. EMT Hedgpeth kept monitoring Todd because she had an uneasy feeling that he was about to "crash."

Within minutes, the deputy sheriff on patrol in the Delmarva precinct drove up to Jeanette Linn's house and came through the front door to the living room. Todd was still reclining on the couch. The deputy approached him as a child approaches a bowl of broccoli: with trepidation and, perhaps, a bit of disdain.

"Hey Toddler, what happened?"

"Some guys jumped me and hit me with a baseball bat."

"Where?"

"On my head."

"I mean where were you when this happened?"

"Can't think."

"When was it?"

"Ohhh – my head," screamed Todd. His head lolled to the left, and his eyes rolled up in their sockets.

Instantly, Hillary was on her radio. "Dispatch, this is Challenger County EMT. This patient we were dispatched to transport is having a crisis. We are going to need to transport via chopper. Put the chopper on alert. We are loading him at the dispatched location now. Our ETA at Delmarva Medical Clinic will be about five minutes."

When the deputy arrived, they asked him to help load Todd on the litter. Hillary, her assistant EMT and the deputy struggled to get a backboard under Todd's bulk. They were finally able to get him into the ambulance.

The deputy went back to the house and called out through the open door, "Mrs. Linn, are you in here?" There was no response. It seemed odd to him that Jeanette wasn't at home or with Todd. The deputy was reluctant to go into her bedroom alone to investigate, but had he done so, he would have found Jeanette Linn in bed, heavily sedated, and breathing shallowly under her oxygen mask.

The EMT's ambulance carrying Todd Linn was speeding toward the medical clinic where the helicopter engine was warming up, and the pilot and a flight nurse were waiting.

"NEPTUNE GEN ER this is Helio Rescuer 2. We are inbound with an ETA of about thirty minutes. We have a thirty-year-old male with possible blunt head trauma, although he has no apparent external signs. He is six feet eight inches tall and weighs about three hundred pounds. He has a mechanical aortic valve and lists warfarin among his medications."

Within minutes, Helio Rescuer 2 was safely secured to the roof helipad at Neptune General Medical Center. Todd was quickly admitted to the

Emergency Department. They tested his International Normalized Ratio (INR), the test for assessing if the correct dosage of warfarin was being given. Todd's INR was quickly determined to be 4.3; not very high by normal standards, but of concern in this case because he was probably bleeding into the brain.

The clerk recording all of this medical data was also attempting to get the information needed for the hospital admission database.

"Mr. Linn, who's your next of kin?"

"Mother"

"What is her name?"

"Jeanette ... can't think of her last name."

"Linn, the same as yours?"

"Yeah."

"Do you want her notified?"

"Not really. Wouldn't make any difference. She can hardly get out of bed without help."

The clerk checked the box indicating that no information was to be released about Todd Linn.

Shortly, Dr. Cunard Lee tried to communicate with Todd. "I'm Dr. Lee, the neurosurgeon whom they called in on the case. You have some bleeding between your skull and your brain. We are going to operate to get the blood out and try to stop the bleeding."

Todd did not respond and showed no signs of consciousness. Dr. Lee had the floor clerk attempt to call the next of kin, but the only information listed on Todd's hospital record was his mother's name – no address or phone number. In addition, Todd wasn't carrying any ID and his only personal item was a pair of pocketless blue shorts. To make matters worse, the admission record appeared to show that Mr. Linn had requested that no information about him be given out. Frustrated, Dr. Lee left an order requesting that the social worker on call try to find Todd's contact information and attempt to get permission to phone the patient's mother.

Given the urgent need, the surgery got underway at eight o'clock on Sunday morning. The surgery team was never able to locate the site of the bleeding and consequently it couldn't be stopped.

Todd Linn was transferred to the Neurological Intensive Care Unit. As the day progressed, his condition continued to worsen and did not give his doctors much hope for a significant recovery. He remained on life support while the hospital repeatedly tried to contact his mother.

Finally, at nine o'clock on Tuesday morning, the hospital attorney had obtained a court order overruling Todd Linn's apparent wish that nobody be informed about his hospitalization. The social worker assigned to Mr. Linn had contacted the Challenger County Sheriff's office about the whereabouts of his next of kin.

The call was put through to Sheriff Pickett, who assured the social worker that he was aware of the case and knew Mrs. Linn. He assured her that he would personally go to her house immediately to inform her of the situation. He also promised he would have Mrs. Linn contact the social worker within the hour.

Despite his promises, the sheriff leisurely delegated the task of contacting Jeanette to his chief deputy, who grudgingly agreed to carry out his boss's wishes.

Forty-five minutes later, Jeanette Linn called the social worker.

"I'm Jeanette Linn."

"Mrs. Linn, I'm so sorry it has taken us this long to contact you. Is Todd Linn your son?"

"Yes."

"When he was admitted to the hospital, he didn't have any ID and said that he didn't want you to be contacted. We had to get a court order to allow us to locate you. Todd is in serious condition. I'll let you talk with his surgeon."

"This is Dr. Cunard Lee at Neptune General Medical Center. Are you Todd Linn's mother?"

"Yes."

"I have been caring for your son since early Sunday morning when he came in with a head injury. When he was admitted, he told the nurse that he had been hit in the head with a beer bottle."

"He told me that it was a tire iron."

"Whatever happened, he lost consciousness soon after I arrived at the hospital. His tests showed that he was bleeding inside his head. I tried to remove the blood clot, but as soon as I did the bleeding got much worse. Evidently the pressure built up by the swelling in his brain was preventing blood from flowing. There was no clear solution as to what to do in this case. He could have died from blood to his brain being cut off or he could have died from the increased bleeding. I performed surgery but was unable to stop the bleeding. We feel there is nothing more we can do for him. We have had him on life support for over thirty-six hours now. All of his vital signs are worsening, and I feel that there is little hope that he will recover. I have had this confirmed by another neurosurgeon. We would like for you to consider giving us your permission to remove him from life support and letting nature take its course."

Jeanette sobbed, barely able to speak. "Todd…always said that he didn't want to be…kept alive by ma...chines."

"So you agree that it would be within his wishes to stop life support?"

"Yes."

"Is there anyone else that you feel you should consult before making the final decision?"

"I'm the only one left."

"Would you like me to keep the life support on until you can get here to see him?"

"How long can you do that for?"

"Well, can you come soon?"

"Of course I'll come as soon as I can. I'm in pretty awful shape. I'm an amputee, and I'm on oxygen, but I'll find someone to bring me."

Jeanette called her friend Virgie to make arrangements to go to the hospital. On Wednesday at nine-thirty in the morning, they drove to the Neptune General and were immediately escorted to the Neurologic Intensive Care Unit. The Unit coordinator paged Dr. Lee.

The charge nurse escorted Jeanette and Virgie into Todd's room. She lowered his bed so that Jeanette could see his face from her wheelchair, and then softly left the room. Virgie stood next to Jeanette, gently patting her on the shoulder. Jeanette quietly traced her finger over her son's cheek, bidding him good-bye.

Dr. Cunard Lee quietly slipped into Todd's room. He asked softly "Mrs. Linn?"

"Yes," Jeanette whispered. Virgie backed out of the room and found a seat in the waiting area where she could see Todd's room.

"I'm so sorry about Todd. By the time we were able to perform surgery on him, there was nothing we could do to save him. Are you still okay with your decision to discontinue life support?"

"Yes," she answered without hesitation.

"That is a brave and humane decision."

"I also would like for Todd to be an organ donor if possible."

"Yes, we can arrange that for transplants and medical research. Thank you for your marvelous gift."

Dr. Lee then wrote the following orders in Mr. Linn's chart: "Remove all artificial life support; Respirator; Arterial line. Maintain EKG monitoring. Follow transplant donation protocol."

Once these instructions were carried out by the medical team, Todd Linn immediately stopped breathing. Fifteen minutes later the EKG monitor emitted a steady beep as the electronic line on the screen went flat. The nurse switched off the machine.

Jeanette Linn sobbed softly as she kissed her son's cheek for the final time.

The team arrived to take Todd's body to surgery for the organ harvesting. Virgie and Jeanette were escorted to a quiet family room.

The doctors wrote final notes in Todd Linn's chart. Since their admission record noted an assault, an autopsy was required for any criminal investigation. The pathologist, whose main interest was the brain, had a relatively easy time coordinating the autopsy with the transplant team's organ harvesting.

Together the teams noted the widely scattered bruises over the torso and extremities, the fatty liver, the Marfan characteristics of the body, and the scar where the aortic valve had been implanted. These notations admittedly called into question whether anyone was certain about which of these medical factors led to Todd's death. Also in question was whether his death was the result of foul play.

Sheriff George Pickett was present at the autopsy review and squirmed in his chair after Dr. Cunard Lee concluded that the factors contributing to Todd Linn's death were still unclear.

The sheriff vowed to himself:

"This case ain't going to go on-and-on."

He knew that the longer the investigation dragged along, the greater the financial burden it would put on the county. He also had no liking for Todd or Jeanette Linn and was not inclined to choose *aways* over a real Delmarvan.

Sheriff Pickett had no control over the autopsy findings and knew of no higher-up hospital official who owed him any favors. He was temporarily stymied – an unfamiliar situation to be in for the usually all-powerful lawman.

10

Friday, July 28 - Friday, August 4, 2000
Delmarva

Alex Everly Mann had nothing against technology. He respected forensics, computer data, electronic surveillance and security and, as a pharmacist and a pharmacy inspector, he was required to stay current with advances in medicine and law enforcement. However, in investigations like this, Alex preferred face-to-face evidence gathering by talking to any eye witnesses who might be reliable.

So he could be closer to the action, Alex had his travel agent, Freda secure him a room with an open-ended check-out date at what she had jokingly called, "The lodging monopoly known as Granny Pickett's Bed and Breakfast."

In truth, there weren't any other motels in the town, and the only restaurant in Delmarva was Pickett's Pub, whose front sign read:

"Lead the Charge to Pickett's Pub.
Great Eats and Drinks!
Cash or local checks only.
If we don't know you, you ain't local!"

Phoebe Pickett (née Tipsword), wife of the sheriff and granddaughter-in-law of Granny Pickett, was the proprietor of the pub. Physically, she was a female version of her husband, and like him, she wore a constant scowl whether business was bad or good and whether she was with friends or *aways*. Although they carried only a limited choice of beers and spirits, Phoebe served acceptable burgers, chili and barbeque. Except for local parties, Pickett's Pub was one of the very few places people could go to eat and drink in public. If you wanted to travel a little beyond Delmarva, you could dine at the Crab Palace in the nearby town of Dollar's Quarter.

It was obvious to Alex that his lodging and dining choices were as slim as his chances of finding the pieces of evidence he sought. He knew that working undercover was out of the question. He had worked cases in many small towns where witnesses were closed-mouthed to *aways*, but kept no secrets among the "real" residents. No one but Jeanette Linn appeared to be sure that Todd's death was anything but an accident.

Alex believed that there were still critical pieces of information that needed to be uncovered before deciding if Todd's death was murder or mishap. If he did, in fact, push Todd that night was Monty aware of the injuries it could have caused a person with Todd's medical condition? Was there any evidence of intent or malice found in Monty's actions against Todd Linn? Where was the mystery *away*? Would his testimony be key to the jury deciding whether or not Monty was guilty of murder? Alex knew that he needed to bring out some of his headier investigative tools to have a chance at answering these questions.

Pickett was a time honored name in Delmarva. Many say that the family dated back to the early settlers. Of most prominence was American Civil War Major General George E. Pickett, who led his army of the Confederacy troops against the Union soldiers during the Battle of Gettysburg. While "Pickett's Charge," as it is called, was ultimately unsuccessful and ended in massive casualties for the confederates, General Pickett was praised for his bravery throughout the South.

That Sheriff George Pickett was a descendant of General George Pickett was never formally proven, and the sheriff never actually came out and said he was, but most folks just figured it to be so. Sheriff Picket actually received a yearly award from the Confederacy Preservation Society for his tireless efforts to glorify and promote the memory of the Confederate States of America. To receive and maintain this award, the sheriff donated three thousand dollars yearly for a scholarship bearing his name. It was given to a college student whose area of study was the history of the Confederacy.

He also went a step further by cautiously raising the Rebel flag to commemorate certain battles won during the American Civil War, or as he called it the "War Between the States" or the "War of Northern Aggression."

However, the county commissioner had gotten hold of a copy of the sheriff's flag flying schedule, and made a point of calling Pickett's office each time to remind him that this was not allowed in Challenger County. Sheriff Pickett rarely, if ever, took down the flag until dusk.

According to Granny, it was logical. "If your name is Tipsword, your kin are Tipswords, and if your name is Pickett, especially George Pickett, then somewhere along the line you're kin to General George Pickett." She paused briefly, thinking of a new subject to talk about. "Now Dana Meade, our district attorney, is another story. Says she's related to Yankee General Meade. Now that's all well and good 'n' all, but I've heard talk that her family added an 'e' to Mead, then claimed that they were his kin."

Major General George G. Meade was commander of the Union Army of the Potomac, and was famous for defeating General George Pickett on the third day of the Battle of Gettysburg. Whether D.A. Meade was, or was not a *real* Meade didn't matter to Dana. She just loved to get Sheriff Pickett riled up when they discussed the war that Dana referred to as the "Southern Rebellion." While the sheriff would ramble on, praising the general's gallant efforts during Pickett's Charge, Dana Meade would give him patronizing smiles. When he finished, Dana would look Sheriff Pickett in the eye and say, "But Sheriff – he lost." She'd shake her head sympathetically, and begin to walk away. Then she'd stop, turn around and say to Sheriff Pickett, "Gosh – and we won! I'm proud to be a Meade."

"You mean an M-e-a-d, not an M-e-a-d-e. There ain't no 'e' at the end of your Mead," growled the sheriff.

Dana Meade giggled and replied, "You can't prove that any more than you can prove General Pickett is your long-lost great, great, great grand daddy."

Even Sheriff George Pickett had to chuckle at her comment.

One of the first things that Alex did after checking-in at Granny's was to seek collaboration with the sheriff's office. He doubted anyone would be around on a Saturday, but he did find a tight-lipped deputy who responded to each of Alex's questions about Todd Linn's death investigation with, "Can't talk about police business, especially with people I don't recognize."

Alex had an equally difficult time when he returned to the office on Monday. He was again stonewalled by local law enforcement when he asked to see the police reports and medical files. Sheriff Pickett refused to meet and had no trouble telling Alex that he was an *away,* and a nosy one on top of it.

Alex was also stonewalled by the local residents when he tried to locate witnesses. Many of them felt that Alex was a potential troublemaker in the pocket of Jeanette Linn. Most had little sympathy for Jeanette when she was pitted against one of their own and just wanted the whole mess to disappear.

The sheriff had hoped that Todd's cremation signaled that the case was closed. To let himself off the hook by backing out of an investigation, the sheriff was known to say, "Some cases just don't ever get solved."

Except for Monty Tipsword who responded to all of Alex's questions with, "Ask the sheriff," the only real living eye-witness to the unfortunate mishap was the shifty *away*, which seemed to have disappeared after his night of partying at the trailer. The sheriff stated that the evidence was inconclusive and ultimately came down to the word of a live local against that of a dead *away*

Sheriff Pickett was up for re-election in 2002, marking his thirtieth year in office, and he didn't want this case to open a can of worms regarding his law enforcement practices. He was also well aware of what he called Jeanette Linn's "bleepin' loan company," which gave her enough leverage to keep the case open and her fingers pointing blame in several directions.

Alex decided to drive out to the alleged scene of the crime to do more face-to-face evidence gathering. His persistence in trying to make contact with the sheriff resulted in a very brief phone conversation with him two days earlier.

Alex thought he'd try one more time to meet with the sheriff in person. He arrived without an appointment at his office in the Challenger County Courthouse. The building was unnecessarily massive and, like the sheriff, was decidedly ostentatious. In late afternoon, the massive structure sparkled as the sun rays ricocheted off its golden dome.

George Pickett continued to justify the cost of constructing and maintaining the edifice by saying, "The county needs visitors to spend money here. We want to feature the culture and achievements that we all hold so dear. The courthouse makes a great first impression, which we all know leads to a powerful lasting impression."

Alex bypassed the administrative assistant's desk and boldly strode through the office door. Alex started to introduce himself, but Sheriff Pickett ignored the extended hand and cut him off abruptly.

"I know who you are and why you're here, Investigator Alex Mann. I just have one question for you." Alex nodded. "Why does Jeanette Linn, or anybody else, feel that they need to bring in an outside investigator? "This is my…our…the people's county, and I think I run a top-notch law enforcement agency with top-notch deputies, including our own investigators. Also, Mr. Mann, I'm related to half the people in the area. I can tell you that time and time again, over my many years in office, whenever I couldn't solve a case, or was accusing the wrong man, one of my cousins would pass me on the street and whisper the name of the real perpetrator. The fact that this has not happened in this case makes me sure that I have it right. It was only an accident."

Alex pointed out that the reason why nobody had whispered the name of the perpetrator was that none of them were at the scene when Todd Linn had fallen. He doubted Sheriff Pickett's claims of the competency of his force, but to allay any suspicions, he told him that he'd often worked as a consultant with police and sheriffs' offices and didn't want any credit. "As far as the press goes, if my name is left out, I've done my job," Alex said proudly.

The sheriff's head suddenly shot up. He hadn't fully considered the amount of publicity, good or bad that might result if the Linn death case went to trial. For the time being, Sheriff Pickett would somewhat cooperate with Alex Mann to placate Mrs. Linn.

Later that day, Alex was allowed to meet and quiz the chief county deputy sheriff who was heading up the Todd Linn investigation. The deputy had worked with Sheriff Pickett for almost eleven years and tried to be the "sincerer" of the two. He remained standing in his small office at the courthouse after asking Alex to be seated.

The deputy spent the first fifteen or so minutes reviewing the information he had gathered from police, emergency medical, hospital, and coroner reports.

Alex found this truly helpful as he familiarized himself with names, locations, and other investigative details. He had a few more questions for the deputy, who answered them curtly, yet truthfully.

"Was the crime scene secured, and if it was, when?"

"Not sure it was a crime scene or if a crime was committed, but 'nope' to your question. By the time we figured out what night Mr. Linn fell down the steps of Monty's – Mr. Tipsword's trailer, three days had passed. Hell, by then a half a dozen locals must've come in and out of that trailer. And, the maintenance guys at the trailer park cut the grass and raked up the woodchip piles the following Monday."

"Who asked them to do that? Why didn't someone tell them to stop? For Chrissake, it was a crime scene!"

"Calm down Mister, or is it Doctor Mann?"

"Mister" is fine. I didn't want to abuse The G.I. Bill."

"Well, the crew is scheduled to do the outdoor maintenance work every Monday. On that Monday, all we knew was that there may have been a fight. At first, we thought that fight happened Saturday night at a place on the docks called Sunny's Wholesale Fishery. Old man Sunny had a birthday party for his boy, Junior, who we call 'Partly Sunny' or 'Partly Cloudy,' depending on his mood on a given day. It wasn't until Wednesday, with the death of Mr. Linn, that we were able to put all the pieces together. Even then we weren't entirely sure that a crime had been committed. If we put crime scene tape around the area of every fight and kept it there for five days, there'd be no place to go in the county."

"Did you collect any fingerprints or DNA evidence?"

"The beer bottles and cans and any other garbage were picked up on Monday morning, and we weren't about to rake through the dump trying to find stuff with fingerprints and forensic materials. Inside the trailer, there would've been dozens of sets of fingerprints left around from the party-goers, friends, kin – and I'll tell you, nobody here wanted to process that nasty bathroom. Get my point? Go explore if you want. It's still all there, and more. I'm sure Monty hasn't cleaned a thing in that trailer."

"Sounds like it was a busy Monday. I guess the evidence, with a little help, just kind of split town."

"What are you implying Mr. Mann? That evidence has been tampered with? Because if you are, I'll…"

"Now you calm down, Deputy. I'm not implying anything of the sort. I'm distressed that key evidence might have been disposed of."

"So am I, but you know about hindsight and all that. You go with the leads you have, and sometimes they come too late to help. Any other questions for me, Mr. Mann?"

"Yeah – What are the locals saying about the case? What's the scuttlebutt?"

"I don't think we're calling it a 'case' yet, just an 'investigation' for now. If you want to know what folks are thinking, why don't you go and ask them?"

"Think they'll talk to me?"

"If you're an *away* and you don't own a loan company then your chances are painfully slim. In any case, that's something I won't be helping you with."

Alex really didn't want the deputy's company anyway. He thought that the lawman's presence would only make the townsfolk more closed-mouthed than they already were. He didn't, however, relish going into a potential lion's den alone either.

After arming himself with the information that he had gathered from Jeanette Linn and the deputy sheriff about Todd's death, Alex planned to visit the Edgewater Trailer and Mobile Home Park the following day.

He arrived mid afternoon, hoping that some residents would be around and would feel like talking. He made a few slow loops around the area, trying to familiarize himself with the twists and turns of the dirt roads that traversed the park. In some places, blowing sand from the nearby beach had nearly obliterated some of the lesser-used roads.

He found Monty's trailer easily, and began snapping photos around the suspected crime scene. Across the road, he noticed a short, slender, middle-aged woman pulling weeds in front of her trailer. She was wearing a once-colorful floppy brimmed sun hat and garden gloves that looked almost like oven mitts. Alex slowly opened the car door and eased out onto the road. He smiled and nodded at her in a friendly manner. She warily eyed him and gave a brief wave of her right hand.

Alex walked towards her and extended his hand. "Hi. Hope you don't think I'm snooping around. Well, to be honest, I am snooping around, but it's legal snooping. I mean the deputy, and I think the sheriff probably know I'm here." His voice trailed off and his cheeks reddened.

The woman was amused that Alex seemed flustered.

"Is it me or Monty's trailer that's got you all 'stuttery'?" She took off her hat, which she used to fan her face before firmly placing it over her gray, beehive-wrapped braids.

Alex thought:

"Great, strike one, I'm acting like a rookie P.I. If it's hard to talk to her, how's it going to be talking to the neighbors who are probably less friendly and less humorous?"

Alex quickly recovered. "Neither," he said in as upbeat a tone as he could muster. "I'm just a little out of practice. I retired a few years ago, and I've been doing too much investigating in front of a computer rather than out beating the bushes."

"Well Mr. Mann, the town's been shook-up a bit since Todd had that accident at Monty's. Everyone in town heard you were coming here to – well – as you yourself called it, to snoop around. Jeanette has been telling anyone that'll listen about how Monty beat up and murdered her son and how she was bringing in a private investigator that'll get her justice."

Alex thought:

"Strike two, Always exchange names from the very beginning. Puts people at ease."

"Please forgive my lack of manners. I didn't introduce myself, but I see you already know my name. I'm Alex Mann, but I didn't ask you your name."

"I'm Charlotte Tipsword – just call me Lottie. I'm Monty's aunt by marriage. Well – my husband's been passed for over five years. I wonder if Monty's still my nephew – I mean legal-like? What about you, Alexander? May I call you Alexander?"

Alex didn't know if he should correct her or not. His given name was simply "Alex," not Alexander, not Alec, not Alexi. He smiled at Lottie and said, "How about Alex? All my friends call me that." Lottie seemed flattered.

"What do I think about Monty still being your nephew?" Alex had thought it was an odd question.

Lottie half-nodded.

"Um, my wife died two years ago. I'm fairly certain that my in-laws are still my in-laws if I want them to be. I think the only way your in-laws can no longer be your in-laws is through divorce. So, I'm pretty sure Monty is your nephew if you want him to be. Now the legal stuff is tricky, like if he was in your will or vice versa." He searched Lottie's eyes for a reaction but saw none. "Is that it, Lottie? Is there a financial matter between you and Monty?"

Lottie looked up quickly and directly into Alex's eyes. "Nope, not counting my pennies – just counting my kin."

Alex wanted Lottie and the rest of the Delmarvans to see him less as an "expert" and more as a concerned friend of the family. In spite of the fact that the Linn's were not popular in Delmarva, they were less of an *away* than Alex was.

Then there was Jeanette's loan company. A few locals called her the "Lender with a Heart" and one even called her "Saint Jeanette" when she gave him a loan to stop the foreclosure on his shack and fishing boat. Some townspeople couldn't ignore her pleas for justice, even if it meant having a real-life trial that would cost the taxpayers money. Then again, it occurred to others that if there were to be a trial, it might bring some reporters, lawyers, witnesses and out-of-town kin to Delmarva. These visitors would be obliged to eat in the local restaurant, sleep at the local bed & breakfast, and feed the parking meters surrounding the courthouse. The town might actually make some money on this whole deal.

Alex felt that things were moving in the right direction with Lottie Tipsword, so he started probing her with questions about what she knew about Todd Linn's death. He noticed that, like the deputy sheriff, she was reticent to call it a murder. "Toddler fell on Monty's steps, but that doesn't make Monty a killer," she told Alex.

"I guess that's true," Alex replied, "But we'll never really know if it was an accident or – well – if a crime was committed unless this 'incident,' as some people are calling it, is further investigated. I need help, Lottie. I need to talk with people who are willing to tell me a lot more than the sheriff and deputy.

"So you think my nephew is guilty, Alex?"

"I didn't say that. I'm not a lawyer or a judge, and I think it's too early for anyone to know what happened. It would really help if we could locate the mystery party-goer. He is certainly a potential key witness."

"Well, I never actually saw him. Maybe my daughter, Juanda – some folks call her 'Tipsy' – did. And other people who went to Monty's party live in this park too. They probably saw him."

Juanda may have been in a quandary about choosing between her boyfriend and her cousin, but Lottie made it clear to Alex and everyone else that she wasn't siding with anyone just quite yet. Like Jeanette and Alex, she was just looking for the truth.

"Lottie – How can I talk to them? I know I'm 'persona non grata' but what will it take?"

Lottie pondered the question for a few moments. "First thing is, tell me what you just said. And not in French this time."

Alex looked contrite and said, "Sorry, my, uh, French is rusty. What I meant was, you know, I'm unwelcome, I'm a snooping *away.*"

"Can you cook?"

"Huh?"

"That's probably your 'in.' Now – can you cook?"

"I'm pretty good actually," Alex said proudly.

"How about mutton?"

Alex looked at her blankly. "Are you sure they would want lamb?"

"Naw – Here, we call any meat 'mutton.' Can you barbeque?"

"Sure, I'll pick up steaks and burgers, and maybe some chicken. If the neighbors would bring some sides, we could have a pretty nice dinner to put them in a talking mood.

"No chicken! Chicken is all that people here eat when they want a change from fish. If you want to open these folks up then you better give them mutton. No chicken," Lottie repeated. "But beer, lots of beer. And soda, real soda – not diet."

"I can, I will. When? What day?" Alex asked excitedly. After some deliberation, Alex and Lottie decided to have the party on Thursday, just two days later. He didn't want to give the residents too long to think about it, and he knew that they would have to go to work the next day so they wouldn't stay too long. Alex hoped just long enough to give him solid evidence for the case.

He left it up to Lottie to ease the town's people into accepting the notion that somehow having dinner with Jeanette Linn's *away* hired hand was a good idea. Basically, the draw of free beer and mutton tipped the scales in favor of throwing out all loyalties to "kith and kin" and indulging oneself. Soon after finishing his conversation with Lottie, Alex drove away, confident that this party would provide him with the break in the investigation he needed.

When people asked Lottie if they had to talk to Alex Mann in order to eat and drink at the barbeque, she reassured them that they could say as much or as little as they wanted. One neighbor who had a tiny trailer about six spaces down faked an awful British accent and said, "Aye – I'll drink the Queen's tea and eat the Queen's crumpets, but nary a word I'll speak." At that, he doubled over with laughter at his own impersonation.

Alex continued to snoop around for clues and took dozens of photos in and around the closed-mouth town. Then, about four o'clock in the afternoon on Thursday, Alex drove back out to Lottie's trailer. In his car were six large coolers spread throughout the trunk, back seat and passenger's front seat. One cooler held the steaks, one held the burgers, two coolers held the cans of soda and the last two held glass bottles of real imported beer – beer actually brewed outside of the U.S.A. In addition, Alex had picked up two chilled kegs of domestic beer. He was almost completely penned into the driver's seat. With each turn he made, the coolers and kegs shifted and pressed up against him. It was a particularly wild ride when he had to negotiate the bumpy, winding dirt roads of the Edgewater Trailer Park.

Alex spent the next hour getting ready for what was promoted as the "almost-impromptu, no-strings-attached barbeque." Lottie had told him to expect about thirty people. Alex predicted more would come as word spread around town, but Lottie was skeptical that even with the free food and beer, some folks would stay away because of their loyalty to Monty Tipsword and their mistrust of *aways.*

Lottie got an earful from some residents who reminded her of what her last name is. “Hey Lottie, it wasn’t Toddler Linn that helped get the fishing business up and running and gave a lot of us jobs on the “Challenger.” It was Monty Tipsword and his father, or we should say, the ‘Godfather’ that did. Now look Lottie, we won’t speak ill of the dead or a dead man’s kin, but that Toddler was slow and lazy. Most everyone knew he was mostly drunk when he wasn’t working.”

It rubbed most of the townsfolk the wrong way that instead of taking care of Jeanette at night, Todd drank beer with Juanda at Lottie’s trailer. Todd usually pretended to listen to Juanda as she recounted her day. Some of it was because they worked together, often alongside each other, so he already knew her day’s events. The other part of it was that Todd wasn’t all that interested in Juanda. He did like her, but he liked her most when she was tipsy. She was much less judgmental of his behavior and didn’t nag him as much once she had finished off a few beers. He liked that she cared about his health and that she encouraged him to see his doctor regularly.

Juanda would jokingly say, “Whether the doctor charges by the pound or the minute, Todd’s checkups must cost a fortune.” Still, she knew that Todd was not interested in being the man of her dreams. For her though, it was better than drinking alone.

Alex had expressed the importance of his trailer park party to Jeanette Linn and, with some reservations; she had given him an acceptable, if not generous, budget with which to work. Just in case more guests showed up at the party than he and Lottie had figured on, Jeanette had allowed Alex to store extra steaks and beer in the spare refrigerator in her garage. Her stipulation was that only he could come to her house to pick up the food. She would not allow anyone near her home that might oppose her in court. Virgie had planned to stay with Jeanette the night of the potluck to make sure that she wasn't bothered by anyone.

Not being familiar with organizing potluck dinners, Alex assumed that someone, hopefully Lottie, had told who to bring what. Maybe they used sign-up sheets: appetizers, salads, desserts, etc. However, no such organization existed. It seemed like the local residents thought that as long as they were getting free mutton and drinks, they wouldn't need to spend much time being creative with potluck fare.

"Besides," some said, "this is really Jeanette's bloodhound's party. Remember, *he* invited *us*. I'll bring something to be neighborly, of course, but I'll be in line for seconds and a doggie bag when the barbeque is over."

Lottie had commandeered five charcoal grills from the surrounding trailer homes. She and Alex arranged them in a large semi-circle on an even gravel patch in the south corner of the grassy common area reserved for this type of event.

They stacked piles of plastic-coated paper plates, jumbo red plastic cups, napkins, real metal forks, spoons and steak knives, as well as small bottles of steak sauce, ketchup and hot sauce on the picnic tables near each grill. They had also set up card tables so guests could set out their potluck dishes. Alex figured they would bring their own serving utensils and whatever else they needed. Some did – some didn't.

The first wave of people came around five-fifteen in the evening. Many had already stopped at Pickett's Pub to fortify themselves with a beer, and ended up being admonished and called traitors by the sheriff before heading off to – who knows what? – at the party.

Alex had stopped at a local home and garden store and bought four large plastic garbage cans. He filled them with ice and bottles of beer and soda, and, at Lottie's suggestion, placed them right at the entrance of the common area. They hoped that their guests would start partying immediately upon arrival. They also hoped that the "coldfeeters" would not up and leave.

Alex got the grills lighted and waited for the coals to whiten while Lottie put out disposable aluminum trays of hamburger buns and packaged dinner rolls. As she made her way through small groups of curious party-goers, Lottie noticed what they had brought for the potluck dishes. There were no salads, or fruit, or cheese and crackers, or salsa and chips, or even desserts. What the party guests brought was seafood: raw, broiled, boiled, baked, and sautéed. Some even brought chicken.

Lottie wasn't about to take the fall for improper planning, but at that moment, she couldn't come up with anyone else to blame. She saw many guests milling around the potluck tables, and as she walked nearer, Lottie heard them grumbling about the food selection, which they called "SOS" ("same old seafood" or, less delicately, "same old shit"). She began quickly roaming around, asking folks if they wanted steaks or burgers, or both, and how they wanted them cooked. Once they told her, Lottie would give each of them a cold beer along with a smile.

Alex hadn't strayed from his post. He stood anxiously at the grills, shifting his weight back and forth, from left foot to right foot. No one had approached him yet, but as the aroma of grilled steaks and hamburgers wafted through the common area, some of the guests started to gravitate towards the grills.

Alex's first contact with the party-goers began as they started giving him advice about the proper way to barbeque. "Only flip the burgers once; sear the steaks on both sides before grilling them; go by color, not by time."

Alex continued to make small talk with some of the guests and tapped both kegs to keep their tongues moving. Suddenly realizing nobody had brought anything for dessert, Alex left Lottie in charge of the grills, and before driving to Swigs Liquors, he asked her if he should pick up coffee while he was shopping. She grinned and told him, "After sundown, the only thing we put in coffee cups is beer."

Alex bought out the store's supply of ice cream and any prepackaged donuts, cookies, and cupcakes he could find. Swigs Buser packed up the ice cream in a box loaded with dry ice, and loaned Alex a pair of cotton work gloves and tongs to help unpack it at the party.

When Alex returned to the party twenty-five minutes later, most of the guests were red-cheeked and laughing from the effects of the unlimited beer and red meat. Despite his fears, Alex was not driven out of town on a rail. In fact, he was beginning to be thought of as down-right approachable; and approach him they did. Alex suspected that the veteran cap he was wearing was working its magic again.

As they lined up at the dessert table, the guests playfully squabbled over who would get stuck with sherbet rather than ice cream. In Delmarva, comparing sherbet to ice cream was like comparing chicken to mutton – no contest, in either case. Soon, they eased into talking to Alex about the town's current events. It started simple – how the prices of bluefish and cod were affecting local fishermen, the problem of finding a good teacher who would stay at Delmarva's elementary school for more than a year or two, weighing in on a rumor that someone had a bright idea to open a sushi bar in town, and of course, each had an opinion about what had happened and who or what killed Todd Linn.

Alex cornered a few of his new "friends" and pressed them a bit harder for potential evidence. He decided to play the devil's advocate and said, "Maybe Toddler just fell down the stairs, passed out drunk on the woodchips, and woke up later. He probably stumbled to his car, and may have had the common sense to sleep in it, rather than to crash it up somewhere between Monty Tipsword's trailer and Jeanette Linn's house."

That's the way everyone in town referred to where Todd lived with his mother: not the Linn house or Jeanette and Todd's house, but "Jeanette Linn's house." Todd Linn used to claim he didn't care what folks called it. He acknowledged that it was she who bought the house, but said, "I'm aboard ship so much it's really like I live on the "Challenger." Most of

Todd's crewmates would point out that *being* aboard and *working* aboard were clearly two different things. Behind his back, they called him a "lazy freak" who didn't nearly pull his weight.

Certain crew members, including Monty Tipsword thought that the captain cut Todd way too much slack. His medical conditions were making Todd increasingly too weak and unsteady to haul in the daily catch and perform his other duties. When the "Challenger" went out on overnight catches further up the peninsula coast, Todd got to sleep in an oversized bed instead of the usual crew hammocks that would never accommodate his considerable height and weight. A few said that Todd's special treatment had less to do with the captain's big heart, and more to do with the demands of a certain woman whose loan company was a major shareholder in Challenger Harbor & Affiliates, Inc., the company that owned the "Challenger."

At the barbeque, Alex continued on with his fictional scenario. "So Toddler wakes up in his car, drives home and sleeps it off the rest of that Saturday. Then he tells his mother that he's going to Sunny's Wholesale Fishery for Sunny's boy, Junior's birthday. He goes, and he gets drunk and gets into fights with guys from the docks. He makes it home from the party the next morning, feels sick and calls the EMTs. I hear Todd got banged over the head a few times and beaten-up pretty good by some bad guys at the Saturday party."

Alex had cast his bait. Better to have them refute any or all details and theories he had offered than to ask them pointed questions that might freeze them.

"That's bull!" said a large, heavily bearded dock worker. "I was at both of them parties, and I didn't see nothing like that. 'Course I left Monty's shindig before ten, but there was no sign of Toddler at Sunny's on Saturday night. I stayed there till the party was over, then they threw me out. I'll tell you like I told the sheriff's office; it was a crummy party. I was surprised that nothing was going on there at Sunny's. No fights or nothing worse than bragging on themselves like they – we – always do. I guess Sunny's kid, "Little Sunshine" or whatever they call Junior was more interested in chewing and spitting than he was drinking and punching on his nineteenth birthday."

Alex countered, "Well then why have guys come forward and told everyone, including the cops that they saw Todd there, and he was fighting? Some even named names."

The dock worker replied, "Taking credit for giving or even seeing a good beating is a powerful draw for some men. Even if it never happened."

A couple of other men agreed with what they heard from the dock worker. When they returned to port, the alleged eyewitnesses, conveniently on a three-day catch, were sure to have foggy memories about what they had told the deputies when originally questioned.

"Okay, I guess I was wrong about my theory," said Alex. "So Todd Linn wasn't at Sunny Junior's party, and there are no reliable people to confirm that they had seen any fights that night at the barbeque. But tell me, where was Toddler later Friday night, well, Saturday morning?"

Lottie walked by at that moment, pushing around a small flower cart loaded with shaved ice and cans of soda. She figured that the guests were drunk enough to talk, and she didn't want them incoherent by the time Alex questioned them. She answered Alex's question herself. "Juanda already told the sheriff's men that she saw Toddler passed out cold by Monty's trailer. She said she covered him up with a light blanket, not because she thought he'd be cold, but to keep off the mosquitoes and black flies. Damn they bite! When I got up around four o'clock – that's when I always get up to feed the cats on the porch – I didn't see Todd laying there, and I didn't see his car either. Let me tell you that there's a spotlight over Monty's door, and I couldn't miss seeing big old Toddler lying there alive or dead. Nope, he wasn't there then. Like you said before, Alex, he probably slept in his car and then went home. Jeanette hasn't said much at all about what happened on Saturday – or Sunday either. She says she's saving what she knows for the trial – Monty's trial, I guess. But nobody's been arrested yet that I know of."

It was very rare for Swigs Buser to close his store early. However, business was slow, and it looked good for him to mingle with his customers outside of work. Swigs lived in a three hundred-fifty-square-foot studio apartment right above Swigs Liquors. His decorating taste ran toward filling every available inch of space with sports banners, cardboard cutouts and other advertising promotional materials he was given by the various beer and liquor vendors.

Alex was pleasantly surprised when Swigs tapped him on the shoulder. They shook hands. Alex said with a stage smile, “Let me guess, you found some more ice cream in the back freezer, and you came all the way out here to hand deliver it. How nice of you!”

“Nope, better than that. I closed up the store early in your honor, Alex.”

“In *my* honor?”

“Yeah – it’s not often that we have a distinguished visitor like yourself in our town.”

“Well thanks, Swigs, but from what I’m hearing, there may be men and women visiting Delmarva one day soon who are a lot more distinguished than I am.”

“I doubt that’s going to happen in the foreseeable future if the Sheriff’s Office is leading the investigation. It’s unbelievable, Alex.”

“What do you mean? What did they do or not do this time?”

“Everyone is asking what happened to Toddler after Monty’s party. I know about that. I was the last person besides Monty to see this mystery witness before he disappeared at the harbor. Most people heard Monty and that *away* speeding all over Delmarva in Toddler’s truck, honking and hollering through the open windows.”

Alex looked puzzled.

“It’s a weird thing they do here called the “Tanked-up Victory Drive.” If you out-drink someone till he passes out, you get to take his vehicle for a while and act crazy. If they have cash, they'll usually head over to my store and buy more beer. If they don't, they'll usually "borrow" some from the passed-out guy's wallet and then come to my store."

"What happened at your store that night? What did they say to you?"

"I said to them, 'Hey – isn't that Todd Linn's truck? I didn't think anyone could drink that monster under the table.' Then both of them kinda smiled, and Monty laughed and said, 'Let's just say he might've had a little help passing out.'"

"Were they both real drunk?"

"Nah – it was weird. Monty was hammered, but it looked like the other guy was kind of faking like he was drunk. It's hard to describe, you just develop a sixth sense about who's bombed and who isn't when you sell as much beer and liquor as I do. Do you think anyone from the Sheriff's Office, like one of his super investigators ever came around to ask me if Monty and this guy had shown up that night? Well the answer is 'no.' They never asked. And I never offered to tell them. That's their job. Come and ask me, I'm not calling you."

Another party-goer who worked at Delmarva Auto & Marine Supply leaned in close to Alex and said he thought he knew what ship the *away* boarded that night when Monty dropped him at the harbor.

"I'll bet he was crewing on the "Queen of Buzzards Bay." That's the fishing boat that took port here that Friday because they blew a water pump a hundred and fifty miles offshore. She limped into the closest harbor they could find, which was Delmarva. I was working that day and met the captain – a guy named Marlin Frisch. He told me they were heading up the coast once they got the boat fixed. I sold him a new marine back-up battery too. I think he said they were out of New Bedford. Anyway, I guess they worked on it all night, and shoved off early Saturday morning."

Alex asked, "The captain never mentioned this mystery man's name, did he?"

"Nope, it never came up. Only reason I remember the captain's name is because he wrote it when he signed the sales invoice. And it's kind of a funny name. You know, Frisch rhymes with fish. I bet if you follow the "Queen of Buzzards Bay," you'll probably find this guy. It's likely he'll have to go with the crew all the way to New Bedford to get his pay. That's a lot of money to lose if he jumps ship."

Alex thanked everyone who had talked with him, and began cleaning up the grounds at around eleven o'clock at night – later than he had hoped, but thrilled with the information he had gotten.

Lottie Tipsword walked up and began helping Alex with the trash bags.

"Alex, it's late, I'll get the rest of this in the morning. Oh, where are you staying? If you don't feel like driving tonight, you can stay here."

Alex's face reddened, and he mumbled that he was staying at Granny's Bed & Breakfast.

Lottie smiled and said, "Well if you change your mind, Juanda and I can share my room and you could sleep in her room."

Relieved, Alex said, "Really, Lottie thanks for the offer, but Granny gets awfully upset if you miss one of her fine breakfasts."

☼

Early the next morning, Alex peered at an over-size windup alarm clock on his bed stand to calculate the three-hour time difference between Eastern and Arizona time zones. He ate a quick breakfast downstairs with one other guest, then went back up to the office that Granny Pickett had kindly allowed Alex to set up in an unused sitting room on the second floor. He picked up the phone and called his long-time friend and sometimes colleague who currently lived in Colorado. Her name is Huyen Nguyen. The name sounds poetic when she says it, but it's almost impossible for a native English speaker to get it just right. She's quickly become known as Win-Win even though she much preferred to be called Winnie.

At the time Alex called her, Winnie was thirty-two years old; petite, with a pretty face and penetrating, alert brown eyes. She sported shoulder-length, silky black hair, but when she was younger, in her quest to be a seen as "real American," she changed its length and color about as often as Alex changes his beard style.

When she answered the phone, he said, "Hey, it's Alex. Do we have a Win-Win situation?"

Alex could hear her groan. "First of all, just call me Winnie, and second, how would I know the status of the situation? You called me, remember? Would you like if said, "You're the man, Mann?" Doesn't it get old?

Alex ignored her comment. "Well, I think I might need your help. We've got a case to investigate. A doozy."

After his call to Winnie, Alex drove to Jeanette Linn's house to discuss the progress he had made in the investigation. Alex told her he was confident that with the help of Win-Win, he could locate and hopefully persuade the mystery witness to return to Delmarva to testify.

"You know I that don't have long, Alex. Do what you need to do."

Alex nodded and tried to reassure her. "Jeanette, I'm right on it. You've got the first team working for you."

"Which reminds me, Alex, tell me more about your partner."

"Winnie? Sure. I met her when she was fresh out of pharmacy school. The pharmacy world was becoming more and more dependent on technology, and they needed specialists to guide them down the road to twenty-first century technology. Winnie was a serious techno-whiz and a perfect fit for the newly-created position, "pharmacist-computer specialist" at the Phoenix office of the Arizona State Board of Pharmacy. I was the senior state pharmacy inspector and gave her on-the-job training which included driving with me around Northern Arizona to make pharmacy compliance checks in towns like Ganado, Payson and Holbrook. This gave Winnie what I hope was a rewarding opportunity to learn the ways of the state board and to demonstrate her technical expertise.

During our training excursions, it seemed like I had shared my whole life story with Winnie, but she hadn't told me much at all about herself. A few weeks later, she seemed more comfortable with me, and revealed some heart-rending tragedies she had faced that had shaped her life.

She was born in Saigon, Vietnam in 1968. Her father had been a lawyer and politician who, along with some of the other old-time politicians, were plotting to overthrow the communist government. The police caught and shot him right in front of Winnie and her family.

Her mother knew they had to leave Viet Nam. Winnie's two sisters had made it out of the country shortly after their father was killed, and relocated to the U.S. Winnie and her mother endured four months of backbreaking work on a government-run farm while they waited for their opportunity to escape. Her mother finally discovered a fairly large quantity of gold that her deceased husband had hidden away when all of their currency was confiscated by the government. She bought Win-Win and herself two spaces on a boat to Thailand. The week-long trip on the dangerously overcrowded boat was harrowing.

Several of the refugees died from extreme heat exposure, dehydration and wounds suffered from a vicious attack by Vietnam pirates who stole all of their possessions. The boat finally limped into a port in Thailand. Eventually, Winnie and her mother made their way to Colorado to join Winnie's two sisters who had settled there."

Jeanette Linn dabbed her eyes with a handkerchief as Alex finished telling her Winnie's moving story. "Well Alex, you're right. She sounds like an incredibly strong, gutsy woman. I'm glad she's working with you...with us."

He told Jeanette that he would keep her informed about any new developments. She seemed a bit more hopeful as Alex began to leave, and she gave him a brief hug. Alex's eyes blazed with commitment. He knew that Jeanette saw him as her last hope.

Alex believed that he and Winnie had mutually benefited from their training trips. Winnie's hands-on experience included learning the procedures for inspecting pharmacies while getting insights into how she could modernize their inventory, recordkeeping and financial accounting. She enjoyed being out in the field and was endlessly entertained by Alex's pharmacy anecdotes. Alex, in turn, saw Winnie in a new light, not just a techno-geek, but given her life challenges, a discerning and strong individual whom Alex felt he could trust in even the toughest situations.

After their update, Alex left Jeanette's house around eight-thirty in the morning. He decided to head over to Delmarva Auto & Marine to see if he could get more on the fishing boat; like where it was headed and to whom it was registered. His "buddy" from last night's barbeque wasn't working that day, but Alex was approached by the owner who seemed like he was expecting him.

"Very little goes on around here that I don't find out about, and besides, the guy you met, my employee, phoned me that you might be coming in today." For the next fifteen minutes, he told Alex all he knew about the distressed fishing vessel.

When he returned to his temporary office at Granny's, Alex Mann made a call to his client. "Jeanette, I have the best information so far in tracking down what actually happened to Todd. The night of the party at Monty Tipsword's trailer, there was a docked distressed fishing boat that had blown a water pump. She's named the "Queen of Buzzards Bay" and owned by the A. Frisch Fish Company of New Bedford, Massachusetts. The captain bought a new pump at Delmarva Auto & Marine Supply. I confirmed with the Harbormaster that the ship spent the night of the party docked here and left the next morning. Well, apparently the repairs were completed overnight. I've never liked conducting investigations in any other manner than face-to-face. I want to go to New Bedford to follow-up."

"We've come this far, Alex. I trust you. Just hurry…please!"

Alex nodded to himself.

"Oh – Alex, I know you've been more than generous with your time, but I'm going to ask a special favor of you. I'd like you to stop by my house for a moment on your way to the airport. There's something I need to give you."

"Of course I will. Once I call my travel agent, I'll let you know about what time I'll stop by."

Next, he called Freda, his ever-improving travel agent from Prescott. "I need a room tonight near Baltimore-Washington International Airport, an early morning flight tomorrow to Boston, a rental car there and a room tomorrow night somewhere around New Bedford, Mass. I'm on an expense account. I don't want the cheapest stuff, but not the most expensive either."

"I'll get back to you ASAP."

"How about if I call you? As soon as we hang up, I have one stop to make here in Delmarva, and then I'm going to be driving to Baltimore. I'll call you in a few hours when I get in the vicinity of BWI."

Alex called Jeanette to let her know that he was on his way to see her. Pressed for time, he debated whether he should leave the car engine running and just dash into the house to pick-up the item Jeanette wanted him to have, or to park and sit down with her for a few minutes. He chose the latter. Virgie greeted him at the front door, leading him to the living room where Jeanette sat in her wheelchair looking toward the fireplace. She asked Alex to bring over a small, decorative urn that sat alongside a variety of cherished mementos on the dark oak mantel.

"These are Todd's ashes. I want to have them scattered, but not here. Not anywhere near Delmarva."

Alex asked, "Have you decided where you would like them scattered? Back in Clarkwood?"

"No, not Clarkwood. It's a toss-up as to which town has given me the worst memories. When you return to Prescott – when you have time – I'd like you to drive up to Sedona and let Todd's ashes float wherever they please over those beautiful red rocks. Todd liked going there. He didn't feel like he was a spectacle when he was surrounded by those majestic mountains."

Nodding his head as he accepted the urn from Jeanette, Alex said, "Of course, I'm honored that you asked me."

Alex made his way to US Highway 50 towards the Chesapeake Bay Bridge and Annapolis. Soon after, he turned north on I-97 toward the BWI airport. At the end of I-195, he turned off into the office park/hotel area surrounding the airport. At the first convenience store, he pulled into the parking lot and called Freda. All of his arrangements had been made exactly as ordered. Alex was happy with his small investigative team and felt that he and Winnie, with Freda's assistance, had a better-than-ever shot at solving the case.

11

Saturday, August 5 - Sunday, August 6, 2000
New Bedford, Massachusetts

The next morning Alex was up early to turn in his rental car and catch his flight to Boston. As he came out of the Boston airport, he thought about the last time he had been to this bustling city. It was in 1992, the 500th Anniversary of Columbus landing in the New World. There had been a parade of tall ships in the harbor, and the traffic had been the worst he had ever seen. Thankfully, the traffic today was lighter. Being a Saturday, Alex was thinking that it was best to call ahead to see if the man he hoped to talk with was at work.

"Yeah?"

"Oh – you're there. Is this Abner – Abner Frisch?"

"Why?"

"I'd like to see you for a few minutes. What time are you open until?

"Probably till about three or three-thirty this afternoon."

"Can you give me a few minutes?"

"I'm busy, but I'll make you a deal. If you can find my place without me telling you how to get here, then we can talk for exactly five minutes."

"Okay, I'll see you soon."

"I won't bet on that."

Through luck and skilled map-reading, Alex found his way to the A. Frisch Fish Company on the harbor near the Whaling Museum in New Bedford. Walking up to the building, it was obvious to Alex that the owners spent their money on something other than building upkeep and beautification. He pushed open a door badly sagging on its hinges and was greeted by a young woman wearing a surprisingly stylish sundress and leather sandals. She drummed her fingers on her metal desk covered in chipped linoleum and eyed him suspiciously.

"I'm looking for Abner Frisch."

Spinning one hundred eighty degrees in her chair, she shouted at the top of her lungs, "Uncle Ab, somebody here to see you."

A minute or two later, a formidable-looking "ancient mariner" entered the office. He had powerful scab-covered hands, an overhanging belly and a shock of grayish-white hair in front that looked like an ocean spray. He wiped his hands on his bloody apron and boomed, "Well – you did find us. I'm Ab Frisch."

Alex started to extend his hand, but thought better of it.

"Nice to meet you. We talked on the phone a while ago. I'm Alex Mann." Using his middle name seemed too pretentious for this setting.

"Can I ask you those questions now?"

"Not now. I'm too busy."

"How about over lunch?"

"Ain't had time for lunch in the past thirty years. But I'll make you another deal. Buy me and my girl here lunch. We'll call and have it delivered. We'll talk while we eat."

"What about our first deal? That one wasn't going to cost me anything."

"We're wasting time, Mr. Mann."

"Okay. Deal."

"Darlin', call and order us a clambake from Lopes. Call me when the chow arrives."

Ab turned and went to back to his work.

Alex went outside to catch some fresh air. The smell of the harbor with its salt water, fish processing facilities and diesel fumes were not what this south westerner enjoyed. He thought:

"Ahhh-give me the smell of sagebrush after a rain any day."

Fortunately, the Lopes Portuguese Seafood Restaurant was close to and a chief customer of the A. Frisch Fish Company, so the meal came quickly.

There was a fish-cleaning counter on the Frisch's dock that the young lady had hosed down and covered with butcher paper. She spread out the clambake, and they began devouring their lunch as soon as it arrived.

Abner Frisch opened the conversation, "What did you want to ask me?"

"I'm a private investigator working on a mysterious death case. Something happened the night that your boat, "Queen of Buzzards Bay" blew its water pump and was in Delmarva for repairs."

"You been working this case pretty hard already, ain't you."

Alex wasn't surprised that Mr. Frisch had already gotten the scoop on him.

"Yeah. There was a party that was breaking up, and there were only three people left at the scene. One was the guy who owned the place, one was a guy who died a few days later – possibly from injuries he got that night – and one was a stranger that nobody could identify. Delmarva is a little town, so it's very strange that a guy could be at a party and have nobody know who he is. I had to figure how someone could be new in town and still get invited to a party. What I came up with was that the guy had to be a fisherman on a boat that spent the night in Challenger Harbor. I checked with the parts store and found your boat's name and registration. I also confirmed with the harbormaster that "the Queen" was there. The captain was Marlin Frisch. Sound familiar? The mystery man's description was about six feet tall, thin, light skin and walked with a kind of rocking motion."

"Darlin', who does that sound like?"

"That miserable, lying, thieving, cheating guy that calls himself Rebar."

"That's what I'm thinking, too," Ab responded.

"Will you help me out and give me what you know about him or do I have to get a subpoena?"

"You mean, take me to court? I ain't got any money to hire one o' those suits to defend me, so I guess we'll have to cooperate.

Darlin', get him the info. I got to get back to work."

Alex followed the young woman as she headed into the office. She forced open the sticky second drawer of a rusty filing cabinet and located the personnel file.

"Reynold Barr – 'Rebar' – quit right after that last trip. He ain't no fisherman. He just walks like one. Whenever he was around, little things were always turning up missing. We sure were glad to see him go before something really bad happened and we had to sic the law on him."

Alex copied down the name, address and social security number for Reynold Barr.

"Thanks much, I owe you one."

"I know, someday. Oh, and thanks for lunch."

Alex drove to his hotel and checked-in. He was anxious to talk with Winnie. A few years before, she had accepted a similar position to the one she held in Arizona and relocated to Colorado to live close to her sisters. There had been several candidates for this job, but a glowing recommendation and a few called-in favors from Alex Everly Mann tipped the scales in her direction.

Winnie called him after she was accepted, and in a sincere, sing-songy voice she inquired, "Alex, I am so grateful for what you did and for having such faith in me, but you didn't lay it on too thick with the Colorado Pharmacy Board, did you?"

Alex laughed and said, "Not any thicker than I had to."

Despite her transfer, Winnie still had access to the National Crime Information Center (NCIC) computer run by the FBI. She and Alex had kept in touch by occasional emails. He called her at work.

"Pharmacy Board, this is Huyen, how may I help you?"

"Do we have a Win-Win situation?"

"I ought to hang up on you Alex. How many times do I have to ask you to call me Winnie?"

"Probably at least once more!"

"I'm just trying to be an American. You know how Americans love winners."

"I know. That's why I call you Win-Win. It sounds like you're a two-time winner."

"Just don't call me a two-timer. What's up?"

"Can you run an NCIC check for me? It's for that suspected murder case I told you about. I'm sure the FBI won't mind if we use their database."

"Sure, give me what you got."

"His name is Reynold Barr." Then Alex gave her the rest of the personal information he had for the possible witness.

Winnie glanced at the report, "Whoa! If I have to print this, I'll probably be written up for wasting paper. This guy has been arrested at least forty times. He has been jailed at least twelve times in eleven different states. Looks like all are misdemeanors: petty theft, possession of stolen property, shoplifting, leaving the scene of an accident, possession of a controlled substance. No wants. No warrants. Looks like nobody wants to expend any resources going after him. His driver's license from Nevada was revoked eight years ago."

"When's the most recent charge?"

"About seven weeks ago in New Bedford, Massachusetts for theft of a six-pack of beer and a carton of cigarettes. He posted bond but failed to appear in court and forfeited it."

"That must have been just before he boarded the fishing boat that ended up in Delmarva for repairs. Guess where I am now?"

"New Bedford?"

"BINGO!"

"You're on the right track but how are you going to figure out where to go next?"

"That's the big question. I don't even know what he looks like. If I sat next to Mr. Barr at breakfast tomorrow, I wouldn't know him. I guess I'll have to go back home to Prescott and wait for him to be arrested again. Could you check on him every day or two and let me know if we get any newer information?"

"Sure."

"Thanks, Winnie, you are a winner."

"Just don't call me a weenie."

Alex phoned Jeanette Linn and filled her in on what he had found. She agreed that there was little else that they could do without a fresher lead. He then called Freda to book him a flight from Boston to Phoenix for the next day. She continued on a roll, getting Alex decent seats on last-minute flights. She also moved him to a hotel closer to the Boston Airport for that evening. Alex told himself that he was not retreating by returning home. He was confident that Winnie would monitor Rebar's criminal activities as best she could by using the crime database.

Alex preferred to characterize his departure from the east coast as a "regrouping" to analyze the evidence he had gathered so far. He hoped that he would not be staying in Prescott for very long. Rebar seemed to be on the run and was sure to soon be involved in his only perceived means of survival – committing crimes.

However, Rebar would prove Alex wrong, and would continue to fly under the radar for four months. Rebar preferred the company of a rig driver in a truck cab to a whole load of people on a bus. He wasn't particularly avoiding anything, but he had grown up on the streets and learned from experience that the fewer people who knew where or who he was, the better off he'd be.

Alex wasn't sure if Rebar had taken a break from committing crimes or was just highly skilled at escaping arrest during a new crime spree. In the meantime, Alex busied himself with local free-lance investigations in Northern Arizona, and waited impatiently for Winnie to call with any news about a Rebar sighting.

Alex had not forgotten the solemn promise he had made to Jeanette. A few weeks after returning to Arizona, he drove up to Red Rock State Park in Sedona, arriving just as it opened at eight o'clock in the morning. When he reached a particularly stunning vista, he uncorked the urn, turned it upside-down and watched as the wind swirled the last remains of Todd Linn. He put the empty urn in his backpack and looked out over the shimmering mountains.

"We'll get to the bottom of this and give your mother the answers she wants so badly. Rest in peace, Todd."

12

Saturday, July 22, 2000
Delmarva

At six o'clock on the morning after the party at Monty Tipsword's home, the "Queen of Buzzards Bay" cast off from the Delmarva docks. Captain Marlin Frisch had mapped a course to take them back to New Bedford, Massachusetts while hitting some decent fishing areas along their way. During periods when they couldn't fish, the crew spent their time cleaning and repairing nets and equipment, as well as telling stories, name-calling and gambling. Nobody had much interest in Rebar, so they didn't notice when he slipped away below deck and searched for any of his shipmates' carelessly secured cash. He usually found a few dollars that he managed to pilfer in their jacket pockets. Rebar was an experienced, crafty petty thief. He never completely cleaned out anyone's pocket. He took about half of the money, leaving the victim uncertain if he had even been robbed. Rebar couldn't make a living at petty theft, but it supplemented his somewhat meager fisherman's income.

Passing under the Highway 611 bridge, "the Queen" entered Sinepuxent Bay and on through the pass at Ocean City where they entered the Atlantic Ocean proper. When they reached the fishing area, Captain Frisch slowed "the Queen" and deployed the nets. The fishing was very good, not excellent, but they hauled in enough bluefish and cod to make each crew member mentally calculate what he was going to do with his money when they got back to home port.

Arriving in New Bedford was one of the happiest times in Reynold Barr's troubled life. He was glad to be off the crowded, bad-smelling, perpetually rocking vessel. He made a vow to himself to never get off dry land again. However, when the A. Frisch Fish company sold the catch, and he collected the largest paycheck of his life, Rebar wasn't absolutely sure that he would keep the vow.

"Hey pal, you need a job?" asked a trucker who had just loaded up with the fish from the "Queen of Buzzards Bay."

"Doing what?"

"I twisted my back yesterday. I need a helper to deliver these fish between here and Fall River. Take us about six hours. I'll give you fifty bucks."

"Make it sixty and you got a helper."

"Climb in."

"What's your name?"

"Rebar."

"Ha! Good one. I used to do some construction work. We poured a lot of concrete and used a lot of rebar. It's strong, bends a little but won't break, eh?

Rebar ignored the comment, "What's our first stop? I'm kinda hungry."

"Fish market over by the mall. Be there in about twenty minutes. There's a C-store next door. You can get something to eat after we deliver."

"Good. I'll sleep on the way. You can't get a decent sleep on a boat. Way too much rocking."

After they unloaded at the first fish market, Rebar went next door to pick up some breakfast sandwiches and coffee. The cashier started to put his purchase into a plastic bag.

"Don't you have a brown paper bag? I hate these plastic things." She transferred the food to a brown bag and Rebar went back to the truck.

The truck rolled west on US Highway 6, making numerous stops at restaurants, small groceries and fish markets along the way to Fall River. At each stop, Rebar caught a short nap while the trucker collected for the delivery and joked with his regular customers. With the truck emptied, they drove to a truck plaza near I-195, and the driver handed him three twenties and wished him luck. Hungry, Rebar headed for the restaurant.

13

August, 2000 - February, 2001
Cross-country, USA

"Win-Win, what's the situation?"

"Winnie, please."

"Winnie, what's the situation?"

"Reynold Barr. Nothing new, sorry. No new wants, no new warrants, but law enforcement still hasn't caught up with him for that bail-jumping stunt he pulled in New Bedford. He could be in a lot of trouble over cigarettes and beer."

"You're a winner anyhow."

"At least I'm not a whiner…'Bye."

Anxious to avoid the coming winter, Rebar decided the time was right to head off to sunny California for Christmas. He had picked up a ride at the truck plaza by offering to throw in twenty dollars for fuel at the next stop.

"Where you headed?" the trucker asked.

"West," replied Rebar.

"I'm going south."

"Good enough. I was on a fishing boat and nearly froze. No more of that. I want warm and dry land. How far south?"

"Got to drop this trailer by Passaic. Let you off at I-80. That's a good way to go west."

"How far is it?"

"Three-and-a-half, maybe four hours. Depends on traffic."

"I'll catch some sleep."

A couple of hours later, while the driver was occupied with the payment at a toll booth, Rebar slipped a leather jacket off its hook and onto the floor behind his seat. This was the first step in getting the driver's jacket out the door when Rebar would be exiting his ride. Reynold Barr remained awake and entertained the driver with stories of his experiences as a fisherman.

The driver guided the big rig into a truck plaza to let Rebar get out. "How about the twenty?"

"What?"

"The twenty you said you'd give me for fuel."

"Oh yeah." Rebar fished around in his pocket and handed the driver a twenty. "I got part of a bag of chips, you want the rest?"

"Sure"

Before the driver could reach them, Rebar dropped the bag on the driver's side floor spilling part of the contents. "Sorry."

"Got to get them crumbs out of here. Can't stand a messy truck." The trucker turned and climbed out of the cab. When the driver's back was turned, Rebar grabbed the leather jacket and climbed out. He laid it on the ground, reached back in for his brown bag, picked up the jacket, slammed the door and was around the truck parked next to them before the driver could get back into the cab and get a final look at Rebar. The driver seemed confused as he shrugged his shoulders and headed out of the truck plaza. Rebar watched him leave, then trotted inside to use the restroom and to get a bite to eat.

Finding a ride west was not easy. At dusk, Rebar decided to walk over to a run-down motel across the road from the truck plaza so he could sleep in a bed for a change. He asked for the cheapest room. In the morning he went back to the truck plaza for breakfast. He struck up conversations with several truckers and finally found one who agreed to give him a ride as far as Toledo in exchange for a too-large leather jacket that Rebar had "won" in a card game.

"Never been to Toledo before. How long's the ride?"

"It'll take us most of the day. Be about dark when we get there."

In late afternoon they arrived at a truck plaza just south of Toledo. Rebar exited empty handed this time.

Across the street from the truck plaza, Rebar could see a large car wash. It was run like an assembly line. You drive in, turn your car over to an attendant who vacuums it, then puts it on the line where it goes through a washer, and finally is taken by another attendant who wipes it dry. This setup allowed Rebar, the master of urban street smarts to hatch a plan. He walked over to the car wash and bought a bag of chips and a soft drink from their vending machines. Then he chose a seat where he could keep an eye on the incoming cars and their drivers. He also watched the doors to the restrooms. A customer went into the men's room just as his car was being driven out to be dried. The trap was sprung. Rebar walked swiftly into the drying area, giving the attendant a fifty dollar bill and a wink and thanks, before climbing into the car and driving away. Reynold Barr was back on I-80 heading west before the car's owner came out of the restroom and discovered that his car was missing.

At the next exit, Rebar paid a toll as he got off the highway. He pulled into a gas station, filled up, and then drove around to the side of the building to use the restroom. When he came back out, he took a better look at the interior of the Chevrolet Prizm he had just "borrowed." In the back seat was a rooftop delivery sign, as well as a polo shirt from the local pizza chain located almost directly across the street. Rebar put the sign on the roof of his car, then slipped the shirt over his own. After a dozen or so people went into the restaurant, Rebar lit-up his sign and drove quickly to the restaurant. As he entered, the crowd was creating chaos – kids were jumping around laughing, the phone was ringing off the wall, and pizzas were ready to be taken from the oven. Three tables were impatiently waving for their waiters. Rebar saw two pizzas in boxes under a heat lamp waiting to be delivered, so he snatched them up and was gone before anyone noticed him. At the first stop light he pulled off the shirt, took the sign off the top of the car, then swung back onto the entrance ramp for I-80 westbound. By this time, the police officer was just arriving at the car wash to take a stolen car report.

After an hour's drive on the Ohio Turnpike, Rebar paid his toll and continued onto the Indiana Toll Road. He faced a dilemma. He needed sleep, but it would be risky to stop at a motel close to the highway. He knew that cops frequently patrolled these places, scanning for license plates for stolen vehicles. They considered it to be equally egregious to steal a license plate from another car. He took a gamble and picked the latter.

Rebar got off at an exit with several apartment complexes around it. He pulled into one of the parking lots to unscrew the rear license plate from *his* car. Then he crossed the road into another complex. After circling about half of the parking lot, he found a car of the same make, model and similar color as his. He quickly removed the plate from the second car and put it on the rear of his car. He didn't bother to change the front plates. He had heard that few cops ever checked there for a match. Rebar then tossed the pizza boxes on the ground and put the delivery sign on the rooftop of the victim's car.

While Rebar was making his getaway, the apartment security officer on patrol spotted him. He hadn't seen the entire operation, just enough to make him draw the wrong conclusion. He called the local cops and reported that he had thwarted a license-plate stealing caper. The responding officer called in the license plate number and confirmed that the car was reported stolen. The officer had the car towed to the impound lot, filed his report and left. It would be the next morning before the superintendent of the impound lot discovered that the front and back plates didn't match and that the VIN went with the plates on the front.

In a cheap motel ten miles away Rebar slept like a baby.

After a leisurely breakfast at a fast-food joint, Rebar continued his trek west. He knew practically nothing of the geography of the United States, but a trucker had told him that if he stayed on I-80 he would eventually arrive in California. For now, he had to settle for Chicagoland instead of La La Land.

The junction of I-80 and I-294 came up too quickly for Rebar to get in the proper lane. Before he could figure out how to correct the mistake he came to the toll plaza. To his right was a monstrous traffic jam. To his left, cars were zipping by. Not knowing about the prepaid toll transponder lanes, he zipped right through one, setting-off flashing red lights from a Cook County Sheriff's Police car. He forced Rebar's car to the side of the road and ran a check on the license number. It took an unusually long time for the results to come back. Indiana's time zone was one hour later than Illinois', and the time difference had given the Indiana impound superintendent just barely long enough to get his report entered into the National Crime Information Computer. Less than a minute after the information was updated, Rebar set an unofficial record for the fastest any suspect had ever been apprehended after his or her data was entered into the NCIC.

"Winnie, what's the situation?"

"Call me – wow, you did. That's better. Let me look. Um, you're in luck. Reynold Barr is in the Cook County, Illinois Detention Center, charged with a whole bunch of things like evading a toll in Illinois, fraudulent use of automobile registration in Indiana, grand theft auto in Ohio, theft by impersonation in Ohio…"

Alex cut in, "You're a winner."

"Except now my boss is on my back for all the times I'm getting on this NCIC computer. She wants to know what I'm up to."

"How did you handle it?"

"I pretty much ignored her."

"Did that work?"

"Don't know yet. I just know that she is not pointing an automatic rifle at me like the cops back in Vietnam. I'm really not worried. She just thinks she's tough. She doesn't even know what tough is. Besides I'm doing my job…sort of."

"If this works out, I'll buy you a steak dinner."

"For a bowl of pho I'd follow you anywhere."

"Phooey!" Click. Alex hung up.

Instantly Alex was back on the phone. A pleasant voice answered, "Challenger County Sheriff's Office."

"I'd like to speak to Sheriff Pickett, please."

"Who's calling?"

"Alex Everly Mann."

She sighed audibly, "One moment, please."

"Investigator Alex Mann, what's happening?"

"Hi Sheriff George Pickett," Alex teased. Our wayward mystery witness is what's happening. Remember him?"

"Mr. Mann, don't sell me short. We run a pretty tight ship here. Of course I remember him."

"Well, his name is Reynold Barr, and he's in the Cook County Detention Center in Illinois. Once he makes bail, he'll probably disappear into thin air again. Can you put a hold on him?"

"Sure."

"I'm going to fly to Chicago today. I'll talk to him tomorrow and see if he'll let me bail him out. I'll bring him to Delmarva to hear what he says happened to Todd Linn at Monty's that night."

"I'll get right on it."

"Thanks, Sheriff."

Alex made another call. "Jeanette, this is Alex. We seem to have had some luck."

"What's that?"

"Reynold Barr, the guy I want to talk to is locked up in a detention center in Chicago."

"How is that good luck?"

"I just hung up with Sheriff Pickett. He agreed to put a hold on him so they won't release Mr. Barr until I get there."

"I'll believe it when I see it."

"Well anyhow, I'm going to fly to Chicago this afternoon and see if Mr. Barr will let me bail him out and come with me to Delmarva tomorrow. I plan on convincing him to tell the good sheriff what he knows about the incident that led to your son's death."

"Do you think that he'll agree to do that?"

"I don't know, but it's our best chance. What if I sweeten the pot and offer him a plane ticket to anywhere in the country he wants to go when this is over?"

"Sure. Let's do what we have to do."

"I'll call you back tomorrow after I talk to him."

Next, Alex was on the phone to Freda. He requested a flight that evening from Phoenix to Chicago. His second request was that she find the location of the Cook County Detention Center and book a hotel in that area. He told Freda that he would call her back when he got to Phoenix. The flight to Chicago was uneventful, and things went almost according to plan. He landed at O'Hare Airport, but she booked him at a hotel near Midway Airport. The taxi ride took over an hour and drained Alex's supply of cash. He didn't check in until very late that night.

Mainly due to bumper-to-bumper traffic on the expressways, it took him longer than expected to get to the detention center the following morning. Alex thought of the joke about morning traffic in Prescott:

"If there are three cars in front of you, it's called a 'jam-up.' If there are four cars in front, it's called 'rush hour.'"

Meanwhile in Delmarva, Sheriff Pickett's data entry clerk had taken sick-time the previous afternoon. This was a key fact that the sheriff hadn't shared with Alex. It meant that the hold request didn't get entered into the crime database.

The state of Ohio's budget cuts had eaten into the local law enforcement's fund for extraditing suspects in non-violent crimes, and they had notified the Cook County District Attorney that they did not wish to extradite Reynold Barr. Also, Indiana was not going to go through the extradition procedure to bring someone charged with changing license plates improperly.

These factors led the Cook County Night Court to charge Reynold Barr only with failure to pay a toll. The fine was substantial and took half of the money that Rebar still had from his fishing stint. Just before midnight, he was released with a harsh warning from the judge who told Rebar that he was on a path to serious trouble. The stolen car was impounded, leaving Rebar with no transportation. He climbed into a taxi waiting for a fare in front of the jail.

"I need a cheap motel."

"Gotcha, Bro."

After a few minutes ride Rebar asked, "What are those lights?"

"Midway."

"What's Midway?"

"An airport."

"I can't afford an airport hotel."

"Gotcha covered, Bro."

The cabbie delivered Rebar to a motel that had a room for considerably less than half the price of the room that Alex Mann was staying in across the street. By nine o'clock in the morning, the two men, who were less than five hundred feet apart, were experiencing far different emotions. Rebar rejoiced in his renewed freedom. Alex was dismayed at the breakdown of the justice system. Rebar hitched a ride back to I-80. Alex booked a flight back to Phoenix.

☼

Rebar's recent close calls with the police made him understandably cautious, and he persuaded himself to lay low again until things cooled down. For over a month, he stayed around the Quad Cities on the Illinois/Iowa border, picking up odd jobs with the kind of employers who pay you "off the books" and aren't interested in inspecting your photo ID card. As his cautiousness subsided, Rebar became increasingly anxious to return to his more lucrative craft.

A few days into February, 2001, Rebar was hanging around another truck plaza, hoping to catch a westbound rig. He needed to use the toilet, and as he was finishing his "duties," someone threw a wallet under the door to his stall. Rebar quickly snatched it up and found that it contained no money. However, there was a driver's license and some credit cards inside. It took him only a second to extract the license and toss the wallet under the dividers. It slid along through several stalls. Figuring that a security officer would soon appear Rebar knew that it was in his best interest to appear casual. He took an unusually long time washing his hands and as if on cue, the expected guest arrived.

"Hey, Sir, I'm from security. You see anybody else in here."

"Guy in a red tee shirt with a white rear of a trailer on it was going out the door just as I came out of the stall." This was true, but Rebar was fairly certain that it was not the guy who ditched the wallet.

Keying his microphone, the security guard said, "I found a wallet in a stall in the main plaza men's room. The suspect might be wearing a red tee shirt with a picture of a truck on the back. There's no money and no driver's license in the wallet, but there are some credit cards in it. I'll bring them to the office."

"10-4."

"Thanks, Sir."

"Sorry I couldn't help you more." Rebar tossed his paper towels into a can, and the urban camouflage master walked out. Soon Rebar had connected with a driver who was westbound on I-80.

"Where you headed?"

"California. I worked on a fishing boat back east, but I puked my guts out and froze my butt off, so now I want to go somewhere warm."

"This eight-oh goes to Cal alright but not to the warm part. Soon as you can, head south to I-70, 40 or even 10. The lower the highway number the faster it gets you to the warmer parts of Cal."

"Thanks for the tip. Where you headed?"

"Omaha or actually Carter Lake, Iowa to be exact."

"How far is that?"

"It takes all day. It'll be dark when we get there. Most of the way is crossing Iowa. People say that it's flat, but it's not. Really it's a bunch of rolling hills." This trucker was more talkative than most. "It's strange about Carter Lake. The border used to be the middle of the Missouri River between Iowa and

Nebraska. Then, a whole bunch of years ago, a flood came and the river channel shifted. It left Carter Lake on the west side of the river, and there still is no bridge going directly from Council Bluffs, Iowa to Carter Lake, Iowa. You have to go through some part of Nebraska to get there."

"Our politicians at work again!"

"There's not much to see for the next ten hours so I'll shut up so you can get some sleep. Oh, can you help me unload when we reach where I'm going? I'll pay you good, and just take a little out for the ride."

"Sure. I'll get some winks in now." The monotonous hum of the engine and tires put Rebar to sleep in minutes. When they pulled into the truck terminal in Carter Lake, Rebar assisted with the unloading and was paid as promised. He used some of the money to get the cheapest motel room that he could near the Omaha airport. The next morning, he set out for the area around the truck terminal to try to find another in the string of rides going west.

It was a few-of-a-kind, warm Midwest pre-spring day in the Iowa-Nebraska area. The following Wednesday would be Valentine's Day. The women of The First Evangelical Church of the Flaming Sword of Salvation, Reformed had put together plates of baked goods to take to older ladies of the congregation who would be unable to attend the services on that day.

One such crusader was out making deliveries, and she made five stops – two in Carter Lake, Iowa and three in Omaha, Nebraska. After the last stop, she went to a drive-thru to get a cup of coffee. When she pulled up to the window to pay, she discovered that she did not have her billfold in her purse. The holy volunteer had used her bank card to withdraw three hundred dollars just after she had started her mission. She knew that she had not left it at home. Embarrassed at her lack of money and frustrated about not finding her billfold, the victim explained her predicament to the clerk. Recognizing her as a regular customer, she gave her the coffee and told her to pay her on her next trip. Perplexed, the kind-hearted church woman thanked the coffee clerk and pulled into the parking lot to call the Carter Lake Police. In a few minutes a police officer arrived on the scene.

"Are you the person who called in the stolen purse report?"

"Yes."

"When did you last see the purse?"

"The last I know for sure was when I used my card to get money at the bank ATM."

"When was that?"

"About eight-thirty this morning. Oh yes, here it is. Look – the bank receipt says eight forty-two."

"It's almost eleven-thirty now. Probably too late to catch the guy. So what did you do after that?"

"I was delivering Valentine's Day treats to the elderly shut-ins from our church."

"Did you take your purse with you each time?"

"No, I didn't take it with me at any stop."

"Did you lock the car each time?"

"No, and I didn't take the keys with me either. I've lived here all my life and have never had any trouble."

The police officer frowned. “Since they opened that new truck stop we’ve been having a lot more trouble. Did you see anyone who looked suspicious?”

“Maybe at one stop.”

“Where was it?”

“I don’t remember. I made five stops.”

“Were you in Iowa or Nebraska?”

“I don’t remember.”

“Do you remember what he looked like?”

“Jeans and a tee shirt. Like every other sinner in the neighborhood.”

“That probably isn’t enough of a description for me to stop everyone I’ll see dressed like that today. Even if I found your driver’s license in his pocket, about the most I could charge him with would be possession of stolen property. We don’t know what state the burglary took place in. The cash couldn’t be proven to belong to you so he would probably use it to make bail and then skip town. About the most you could hope for would be to get your license and cards back. I’ll keep my eyes open but don’t get your hopes up. You should go to the bank and cancel the card and get a new one right away. Then go report your driver’s license stolen and get a replacement. Sorry I can’t do much else.”

“I guess it’s true what they say about doing a good deed and getting punished for it. At least until our eternal father touches us with the flaming sword on the last day.”

Re-entering a stall in the truck plaza restroom, Rebar reveled in counting his newfound fortune. He emerged and waited outside for about fifteen minutes before finding a ride on a rig to Denver. They were pulling out of the plaza just as a Carter Lake Police car pulled in. Rebar looked back and slowly exhaled.

"How long does it take to get to Denver?"

"It'll be dark by the time we get there."

"I want to get to the warm part of California. A guy back around Chicago said I had to get south of I-80 if I wanted to be warm. Is that true?"

"Yep."

"Is Denver south of 80?"

"Yeah, but you probably want to get on down to I-10 or even I-8 to be really warm."

"But Denver is on the way, right?"

"Right. You probably want to find someone in Denver going south on I-25 to ABQ or El Paso."

"What's ABQ?"

"Albuquerque, New Mexico."

"I don't want Mexico. I'm not running from the law."

"ABQ ain't in Mexico. It's New Mexico. That's part of the good old US of A."

"Okay, maybe I'll close my eyes for a while."

After what seemed like an eternity of rolling hills and a treeless landscape, the eighteen-wheeler rolled into the freight depot on Smith Road in Denver. The driver requested the money for fuel that they had agreed upon earlier. As Rebar reached for his wallet, the trucker offered him a hundred bucks to help him unload the cargo.

Rebar nodded that he would help. "Why don't you just take the twenty-five dollars out of the hundred you're going to pay me?"

"Naw – they're two different things. Two different pockets. How do I know you won't skip out and not unload? Then I'd be out twenty-five bucks."

Rebar shrugged and reluctantly gave the driver the money. Once they finished stacking the truck's seemingly endless cargo on the pallets, Rebar followed the trucker back outside the dock yard which was surrounded by a twenty-foot, barbed wire-topped chain link fence. "Well, honest pay for honest work, huh?"

The driver walked towards his truck, then pointed to the security gate. He told Rebar that the guard stationed there would lead him to the office to get his money for unloading.

"Are you kidding me? I thought you said it would be quick cash."

"That's right. That's why you need to go to the office – so you can get cash. Otherwise, they'll mail you a check."

"A *check*…in the *mail*? For a hundred dollars?" Before Rebar could further object to this arrangement, the trucker drove off in his rig. Rebar walked back to the gate and explained to the guard about his deal with the trucker.

"I don't care what he promised you. There's no way I'm letting you back into the cargo yard. We have top security here. Besides, we pay the driver, not the drifter."

Rebar knew he had just lost out on a hard-earned hundred dollars and was angry with himself for being duped by two amateur swindlers. He was forced to set out on foot.

"Can you at least tell me which way is west?" Rebar asked.

"That way," pointed the guard.

"Thanks for nothing. Looks like I'll have to walk to California."

Two miles from the truck depot, Rebar caught a city bus which took him into a less affluent area of Denver. At the next stop, Rebar hopped off and soon located a watering hole with local live music and dim lighting. It seemed like his kind of place.

"What are you going to have?"

"Biggest brew you got on tap." Instantly, Rebar started scrutinizing the clientele – Who might have money. Who might like companionship. Money was usually his top priority, but despite being swindled, he was pretty well set in that department and it had been a long time since he had shared company with a woman.

Being the new guy, he thought it best if he just nursed his beer awhile and waited to see what developed.

A heavily made-up woman in a short, tight cowgirl outfit approached him and smiled as she climbed onto the stool next to Rebar's.

"Most of the strangers we see in here are wearing cowboy hats."

"I don't have a cowboy hat because I'm a fisherman."

"A fisherman? What do you catch, carp in Cherry Creek?"

"Nope, big stuff – deep sea fishing."

"Well Mr. Fisherman, you've got a big one nibbling right now."

Rebar was relishing his good fortune.

"Sweetie, you get back over here," a drunken male voice called out. Rather than moving back toward the voice, she leaned-in closer to Rebar.

"What's your name, Fisherman?"

"Rebar."

"Rebar? That's a good name."

"If you know what's good for you, you'll leave my woman alone," threatened a large, unshaven drunk.

"I'm not your woman tonight. I got me a piece of Rebar."

The drunk got up and staggered over towards his rival. He took a swing at Rebar but lost his balance and fell to the floor. Most of the patrons erupted in laughter. Rebar slipped his arm around his catch-of-the-day, "Let's get out of here."

As they turned toward the door, the drunk on the floor slashed Rebar's leg with a hunting knife. The other patrons panicked, and a police officer sitting in his double-parked squad car heard the commotion coming from the bar. He ran across the street. "What happened?"

The bartender had years of experience dealing with situations like this and knew that it was better for his bottom line if he always took the side of his regulars against strangers. "Argument over a woman." Pointing to Rebar he said, "This guy sucker-punched that guy there in the stomach. He was going to stomp him, but the guy on the floor used his knife to protect himself."

"Anybody else see what happened?"

Someone yelled, "Just like that!"

"Yeah!" echoed the voices of the regulars.

The drunk's girlfriend just sat in stunned silence. She couldn't decide if it was better to tell the truth and try to save her fun for the night, or just to nod her head and stick with her boyfriend. She never had time to decide. When the ambulance arrived, the paramedics scooped up Rebar and raced him to the nearest hospital emergency room, grimly called the "Knife and Gun Club" by the locals. Rebar had just failed his first attempt at urban camouflage in the west.

The police officer accompanied Rebar. With probable cause, he searched Rebar's belongings.

"What's your name?"

"Barr, Reynold Barr."

"I see that ID, it's long-since expired, but what's this one?"

"Found it in a restroom."

"Where?"

"Ohio, Iowa, Idaho, I don't know. I just found it."

"Why did you keep it?"

"I thought it might be a get-out-of-jail-free card."

"Wrong! It's a get-*into*-jail-free card. I'm going to charge you with assault in the bar incident. I doubt that the bartender and customers were telling the truth. Lots of strangers get hurt in there, but they did swear that you started it. The DA will probably decide that there isn't enough evidence to get a conviction and drop the charges, but we've got an assistant DA who hates false ID carriers. She'll probably prosecute that charge. Soon as they finish stitching you up you'll be under arrest. Right now you are just being detained."

"Why not arrest me now?"

"Because once you're arrested the city is responsible for your medical bills. If I wait until the hospital releases you, then you are responsible for the bill. This bad economy has hit everybody hard."

By two o'clock in the morning, Rebar was in the lock-up.

"Win-Win, what's the situation?"

"Sorry, she isn't in today. You'll have to talk to Winnie."

"Okay. What do you know?"

"Let's see... Mr. Reynold Barr is a guest of the City and County of Denver."

"Really?"

"That's what it says here."

"What is he charged with?"

"Assault, possession of false identification, possession of stolen property. Good chance that he will bond out this morning."

"Can we keep that from happening?"

"Can I lose my job? Will your rich benefactor take care of me?"

"I don't know, but will you do it?"

"Already done. I keep telling you I can face down any bureaucrat."

"I owe you two bowls of pho."

"You owe me a tankful of pho. What are you going to do now?"

"I'm going to catch a plane to Denver. With luck, I'll be able to talk Mr. Barr into letting me bail him this afternoon. I'll take him back to Delmarva so that he can testify about what happened to Todd Linn at the party."

"Don't forget to let me know before you go into the jail so that I can remove his hold. Otherwise, you aren't going to be able to bail him out."

"Yes! Right!" sighed Alex. Another one of many important details he needed to remember.

Alex headed out to the Prescott airport, Ernest A. Love Field. There was a plane about to leave for Denver, and there was a seat available. He hadn't even had time to pack any luggage. He simply had to get to Denver ASAP. The small turboprop plane was slow, and the ride was bumpy, but he would be in Denver in about the same amount of time that it would have taken to drive to the Phoenix airport and gone through security.

The plane taxied to a stop on Concourse A at Denver International. Alex didn't want to waste time renting a car, so he caught a cab to the Denver jail and called his trusted friend.

"Winnie, what's the situation?" He didn't want to lose time doing the Win-Win routine.

"I'm in big trouble. I guess my boss has been watching my every move. She made me release the hold on Mr. Barr. Right now they're preparing the paperwork for my suspension. I hope that the jail didn't release him already."

"What are you going to do, Winnie?"

"Threaten them. I'm going to tell them that if they suspend me, they should be ready for a TV news investigation to expose how much time they have spent shopping and watching porn on the state's time. I'll show them that even though I did something wrong, I did it for noble reasons and that I haven't wasted nearly as much of the taxpayers' money as they have. Everybody up through the department director better be ready for possible prosecution. These jokers never even registered for Intimidation 101, let alone passed the course."

"Sounds like a plan, but a dangerous one for your career. I'm going to rush right over to the jail to try to see Mr. Barr. I'll let you know."

"Alex, I'll meet you there in twenty minutes."

"Are you crazy? Even with your threats, they'll fire you for sure."

"I'll take that chance. I'll have my mobile phone on."

"Winnie, I don't like this idea, but I might really need your help."

"Right. Bye."

Now, Alex Everly Mann faced his own bureaucratic quagmire. The jail officials didn't like a private investigator showing up unannounced to see an inmate. Alex had no legal standing in the matter, and now, with Winnie's job status in jeopardy, he didn't know how much of a help she would really be. While he was discussing the situation with the jail administrator, Reynold Barr was facing the judge in a bail hearing.

Apparently, no one there had been notified that one of the Colorado Board of Pharmacy inspectors had over-stepped her authority, misused department files and law enforcement databases, and, in all, tampered with the Reynold Barr case. The judge proceeded with the hearing and set bond at five thousand dollars. Rebar couldn't come up with the ten percent – five hundred dollars in cash – which he needed to bail himself out. He only had about three hundred dollars left from his various jobs, so he was sent back to the holding cell.

Winnie arrived at the lockup just as Rebar's bond hearing ended. She exchanged pleasantries with a law enforcement officer and an attorney who had been in the courtroom. They both recognized her and quietly got her up to speed on Rebar's situation.

The negotiations between Alex and the jail administrator were intensifying as Winnie, without knocking, entered the office. With her biggest smile, she greeted the jail official by name. He scrutinized Winnie for a moment, and then mumbled something like, "long time no see, and what brings you here on this particular day?" Winnie and Alex searched his eyes to see if he may have just received word about Winnie's fall from grace, but detected nothing. Alex told Winnie that they had reached an impasse, so she asked if she could add her two cents to the discussion.

The jail official shrugged and nodded towards Winnie. She began, "What is Mr. Barr's status now?"

"He failed to make bail. He'll go to the 'awaiting trial' unit."

"How long will he be there?"

"At least a couple of weeks. As transient as he is, it's unlikely that any bail bondsman will want to take a chance on him."

"That will cost you a fair amount of money, won't it?" asked Winnie

"Yeah, I guess."

"The crime he's most likely to be convicted on didn't even really take place in Colorado."

"True."

"They'll probably not prosecute on the assault charge since those thugs down on Tavern Row don't want to go anywhere near a courtroom. We both know they'd never show up to testify against Mr. Barr."

"True."

"If we can get him to allow us to bond him out, Alex will take him back East to testify in what we hope is a murder trial."

"So he would forfeit his bond?"

"Yep. Not a real big deal, but Denver would be up five hundred dollars on his bond and would save the cost of his upkeep for two weeks. That should help your bottom line."

"Jails don't run on bottom lines. We aren't in the business of making money."

"I disagree. You do have a budget. You might even get an award for keeping your jail under budget if you can work a few more deals like this."

"I don't know about that, but okay, I'll have him brought to the visitor's room where you can talk."

Alex Everly Mann went in the room first, and finally met Reynold Barr for the first time.

"I'm a private investigator representing Jeanette Linn."

"Who's that?"

"Do you remember the big guy who was drunk at the party the night your fishing boat was stranded in Delmarva?"

"Maybe."

"Well, he died a few days later. My client is, or I should say 'was' his mother."

"What did he die from?"

"A head injury."

"How'd he get that?"

"When he fell or was pushed down the stairs."

"I never touched the guy."

"I don't think that you did, but what about the guy who owned the trailer?"

"Oh, he definitely did. Gave him a hard shove right in the middle of his back. The guy was already struggling to stay on his feet. That wrecked his balance, and down he went."

"Did you see him hit his head?"

"Yeah, real hard, right on that pile of wood chips."

"You're sure?"

"Yeah."

"Would you testify to that?"

"I don't know about that. Me and judges are like diesel fuel and a lighted cigar."

"I could cut you a deal."

Rebar felt like the walls were closing in on him, and he wasn't prepared to put his faith in a stranger who was alleging he could help him. "Nope, I'm not interested."

"Don't you want to hear the deal before you say no?"

"No way, I said I'm not interested."

Exasperated, Alex stepped out of the room and into the hallway where Winnie was waiting. He threw up his hands and groaned, "I'm getting nowhere with him. He's gun-shy about testifying and won't talk about a deal."

"Let me try," Winnie offered. "We're running out of time! We need to try everything we can to convince him."

Alex gave Winnie the go-ahead, and she confidently strode into the room. She warmly shook Rebar's hand and commented on his powerful grip.

"You're perfect," she said, beaming at him with admiration."

"Perfect for what?" Rebar asked cautiously.

"Our client is a very sick woman. She needs someone to take care of her almost around the clock. She has some money, not rich, but not poor either. She's given Mr. Mann permission to bail you out of here, pay your way back to Delmarva, and hire you to help take care of her. Things like household repairs, drive her to doctor's appointments – things like that. She has a woman who helps with her personal needs, but she needs someone for heavy lifting. You know, a young man who's strong like you. You'd be crazy to pass up this deal."

"How much?"

"Twice what a fisherman makes."

"How does she know how much they make?"

"Her son was a fisherman."

"What if they decide to charge me with the crime?"

"It's a slight possibility. If it happens, she'll get you the best lawyer available."

"What if they decide to hold me in jail as a material witness?"

"You still get paid."

"Really? I could make twice what I did on that miserable fishing boat by just sitting in jail and playing cards?"

"That's the deal she has authorized us to offer you. Mr. Mann has known her for several years. She is a fair woman who keeps her word. She wants to see the guy that she is convinced killed her son get convicted before she dies. I think that's the only thing that's keeping her alive. Deal?"

"Mmmmm."

"I've got one more prize to offer you if you stick with us until the trial is over – a first class airline ticket to anywhere you want. C'mon Mr. Barr, do we have a deal?"

"Deal." They shook hands.

"Okay, I'll make arrangements for your bail."

Rebar was "free," and Alex was on the phone with Freda making arrangements to fly from Denver to Baltimore and then rent a car to drive to Delmarva. Two men traveling together with hastily arranged flights, almost no luggage and no return ticket set off alerts at the security checkpoint at DIA. The extensive questioning and searching of Alex and Rebar yielded nothing of a suspicious nature, so they were released. They found their exit row seats and tried to look attentive as the flight attendant went over the plane's safety procedures. Ten minutes after takeoff, Alex went to work. He relied on his people skills to form connections during investigations. He hoped his communication techniques would be effective on Rebar.

"Where are you from, Mr. Barr?"

"I don't really know."

"Were you adopted?"

"Not really."

"In foster care?"

"Not really."

Alex decided to outwait Rebar to see what he would say without prodding. There was at least twenty minutes of silence before Rebar volunteered any personal information.

"I think I was a heroin baby. I've been able to piece the story together from people I've talked to, but over the years, I've left out some parts and filled in others."

"Interesting."

"Many times I've wondered if my birth mother even knew that I was born."

"How would she not know?"

"Supposedly she was high for days, and I was born when she was really out of it. Someone called an ambulance, but I came first. A different woman grabbed me up and ran off. When the medics got there, I was gone. She probably hid me somewhere even the cops don't like to go. I think I had been traded for drugs or whatever like I was money. I remember a lot of people, a lot of houses and a lot of cities. I never really even had a name – the men mostly called me 'Shithead' and the women called me 'Lovey.' I went with whoever would feed me. The earliest I remember was one night when I was about five. A bunch of guys were high, and one gave me a bullet and told me it was candy. I swallowed it and started choking. The woman who 'owned' me at that time became hysterical and took me to the hospital. That was when they discovered that there wasn't any official paperwork on me. It was like I didn't exist. A few days after the surgery to remove the bullet from my stomach, I had to go to court with the woman, who asked that I call her 'Mother.'"

I remember the judge telling her that I had to have a name. She had gotten me in a drug trade at Reynold's Bar and Grill, so she pulled that name out of the air and called me Reynold Barr. The judge gave me a birthday and awarded my 'mother' custody if she worked closely with Child Protection Services. I even went to school for a while. I wanted to be like the kids who brought lunch to school that their mothers had packed in small, brown paper bags. The rest of us got free lunches on a tray. I still like to eat food out of brown paper bags. It helps me believe I have someone who cares about me."

"Wow," said Alex, "I've heard a lot of life stories, but yours is right up there with the best of them. I hope that you feel like telling me more."

"I've been working for longer than I can remember. I've learned that it's easier to stay out of trouble than it is to get out of it. I never ran when the cops were looking for someone. Sometimes I gave them false information. I try to never argue with anyone. You get into an argument, and the next thing you know there's a fight and the cops come. I just agree with anyone and then go and do it my way anyhow. I look for where trouble is starting and get away before it gets ugly. I never wear flashy colors – only gray, brown or blue. You wear red, the next thing you know you're a target. You ever hear anyone say, 'I remember the guy was wearing a brown shirt?' No, they always pick out the guy who is easy to spot.

I never get high – never get drunk in public. Maybe I act like I am, but the guy who's sober always has the advantage. I've made a lot of money pulling things over on people when they're drunk or high. I'm quick like a magician. I never take all the money from a guy's wallet. A lot of times after I take a bunch of his cash, I give the guy his wallet back. I tell him he dropped it. He's too drunk to remember. He looks in it and sees a couple of twenties and by the time he figures out he's short, I'm gone.

'What was he wearing?' the cops ask.

'Red shirt, they always remember. Brown or gray shirt, hardly ever.'"

Both Alex and Rebar became quiet, and then dozed off during the remainder of the flight. They were awakened when the cockpit announced that the plane would be landing shortly at Baltimore-Washington International Airport. They caught the shuttle bus from the airport terminal and rode down to the rental car facility.

As they pulled out of the garage, Alex looked at his watch. "I'm hungry. You like Northern Italian food?" he asked Reynold Barr.

"What do you mean?"

"I was thinking that we ought to stop at a nice restaurant and get something to eat before we wind up at someplace like Pickett's in Delmarva."

"Who's paying and what's Northern Italian?"

"Our employer is paying, Mr. Barr, and around here, Northern Italian is mainly fresh seafood."

"I'm not crazy about eating more of what I just broke my back pulling out of the water, but I'll eat whatever somebody else is buying."

In a few minutes, they were greeted with a cheery, “Good evening gentlemen,” as the maître‘d escorted them to a table.

“White table cloths! I couldn’t have gotten hired as a dishwasher at a place like this.”

“Your life is about to change, Mr. Barr.”

“Mr. Barr! That’s a big change from Shithead.”

“From now on if someone calls you Shithead it had better be MISTER Shithead.”

“That’ll be the day.” Rebar stood up. “I got to use the head.”

Alex took the opportunity to call Jeanette Linn. “We’re on the ground. Mr. Barr went to the restroom, so I’m calling to let you know that we’re on the way. We stopped in a nice Italian restaurant. I want him to get a taste of the good life so he won’t skip out on us.”

“Good idea. Do whatever it takes. It looks like Mr. Barr is our last hope.”

“We’ll see you in the morning. Good-bye.”

Rebar returned to the table. Alex had cioppino and Rebar had crab cakes with an Italian sauce. They shared a bottle of wine. “I could get used to this,” gushed Rebar.

“You probably will get used to this.”

“What makes you say that?”

“You have ‘knowledge.’ Knowledge is ‘power.’ Power brings money.”

“What do you mean?”

“You are the only one besides Mr. Tipsword who knows what happened that night. That gives you power and Mrs. Linn is willing to pay you to use that power.”

"You mean that I'm going to get paid for what I already know instead of what scam I can come up with?"

"Yeah – that's right. There are millions of guys with scams, but only two people in the world who know what you know. Guys who have knowledge have people fighting over them."

"You mean you think the party-guy's lawyer might make me an offer too?"

Alex's face tightened. "I don't know about that, Mr. Barr, but look – this isn't a scam. I just want you to tell the truth. Mrs. Linn and Mr. Tipsword have a great deal at stake here. Just tell the court what you saw."

Rebar nodded his head. Alex couldn't tell if he was nodding that he understood the request or if he was acknowledging that he would comply with it. After dinner, they drove a few miles down the road to a high-end motel chain. Alex hadn't had time to pack anything from home before rushing out to Colorado, and Rebar didn't own anything worth packing. The desk clerk supplied them with some basic toiletries and told them where they could find a men's clothing store in the morning.

Rebar was in bed in the darkened room, but he couldn't sleep. What happened to him was almost beyond belief. He had gone from a homeless drifter in a Colorado jail to a man sought after and pampered because of what he knew. Still, this new life was foreign to him. He asked himself many questions:

"Should he just walk out of the hotel and be a free man?" Free, but he didn't know where he would he go.

"Hitchhike back across the country?" That just seemed like more of the same.

"Go back to fishing?" That was even worse.

"Work for Mrs. Linn?" It was a weird setup, but the pay would be good.

For now, going back to Delmarva with Alex might be the safest thing, especially if he was charged with the Mr. Linn's death. Alex had already agreed to get Rebar a good lawyer if necessary. Knowing that he had tried the patience of the legal systems in several states, Reynold Barr was certain that if he stayed on the run, he was sure to be caught, arrested, convicted and sentenced without mercy. Besides, he felt he couldn't bring himself to run from the man who called him a 'powerful person.'

His thoughts shifted to the incident at Monty Tipsword's trailer party. Over and over he reviewed the details until he had every single one straight in his head. With little sleep, Rebar was awakened by his eight o'clock wake-up call.

Alex planned to be home by the next evening, so he only bought a few items at the menswear shop. He helped Rebar select upscale clothing items, including a suit, two sports jackets, three dress shirts, two neckties and a pair of Italian loafers. He wanted Rebar to look presentable and credible to both Mrs. Linn and the Delmarvans.

They drove the rest of the short trip to Delmarva. Alex advised Rebar of the severity of Mrs. Linn's physical condition to prepare him for seeing her emaciated figure.

Jeanette Linn and Alex Mann sat down with Reynold Barr to explain their plan to force a trial in the death of Todd Linn.

"What do you want me to do, Mrs. Linn?"

"You know that I'm taking a risk hiring you."

"So am I. I don't want to end up in prison."

"Do you have a driver's license?"

"No, Ma'am. Mine was taken away."

Alex spoke up, "I can have my associate, Winnie, pull a few computer strings and remove the conviction that got your license revoked. I'll call her after we finish here."

Alex wondered if the Colorado Pharmacy Board had taken any corrective action against Winnie, or if she was even still employed there. He suddenly checked his wristwatch, "Mr. Barr, we need to rush down to the county courthouse before Sheriff Pickett knows you're in town and interferes with your passing the driver's test for your license." Rebar nodded in agreement.

"A few more questions, Mr. Barr," Jeanette continued. "Could you lift me into a car and back out to my wheelchair?"

"Yes, Ma'am."

"Will you stick with me at least until the trial is over?"

"Yes, Ma'am."

"Would you be willing to stay in my son's old room?"

"Yes, Ma'am."

"Is twice a fisherman's pay enough for you?"

"Yes, Ma'am."

"You know that Alex has background-checked you. You've got more entries on your police record than I can count, but not a single one of them was for a violent crime. I'll take the risk. You're hired."

"Thank you, Ma'am. And Mrs. Linn – I would never lay a hand on you or anyone else."

Alex called Winnie and was relieved that she was still employed. She agreed to fix the records so Rebar could get a driver's license. By the time they arrived at the Challenger County Department of Motor Vehicles, the stage was set, and Rebar breezed though both the written and the "behind the wheel" driver's tests.

Jubilantly returning to Jeanette Linn's house, Alex felt reassured that Rebar would follow through with his promises until the end of the trial. "I'm going to head back to Arizona for now. I'll keep in touch."

"Okay Alex, thanks for everything you've done for me," said Jeanette sincerely.

"Call me if you need anything else."

"Thanks for everything, Mr. Mann."

"Mr. Barr, just remember what I told you about 'knowledge.'"

"Yes, Sir."

Jeanette turned to Rebar and directed him to his upstairs bedroom. "As soon as you get unpacked let's get me loaded into the car. I want to go directly to Sheriff Pickett's office. I want to put more pressure on him now that I have a material witness to my son's death. Be sure to wear that suit. I want you to look more professional than our miserable sheriff."

"Yes, Ma'am."

Ten minutes later, Rebar was packing Jeanette, her wheelchair, oxygen tank and other odds and ends into the car. Rebar drove the short trip to the Challenger County Court House.

Rebar unloaded all the goods and Mrs. Linn in the approximate reverse order that he had loaded them a few minutes before.

"May I help you, Mrs. Linn?" asked Sheriff Pickett's receptionist when they arrived.

"I'm here to see the sheriff about my son's death." This was not the first time that the receptionist had heard this – it was more likely the tenth or twentieth time.

"He has his staff meeting going on right now."

"He never has time to see me, but this time we'll wait." She turned to Rebar, "Mr. Barr would you please go over to Pickett's Pub and get us both coffee and donuts? The sheriff is in there having his breakfast at the taxpayers' expense while we have to buy our own from his wife. Not fair is it?"

"No, Ma'am."

"Oh here, take cash. Pickett's won't let you charge."

Rebar was back in a few minutes juggling a paper bag and two paper cups of coffee. Sheriff Pickett was doing everything he could to extend his mythical staff meeting. He had seen Jeanette arrive and dreaded the inevitable conversation she would want to have with him.

After eating the donuts, Rebar and Jeanette Linn began to lay siege to the office. Jeanette was doing everything she could to make the job more difficult for the receptionist. When she would start clicking away at the keyboard, Jeanette would ask for a tissue. When the phone rang, Jeanette would turn her oxygen flow rate down so that the hissing was softer and she could eavesdrop. When she walked over to an open window to have a quick smoke, Jeanette reminded her that she had oxygen running and that she might burn the courthouse down.

The receptionist thought that the well-dressed, well-groomed Rebar looked appealing and kept sneaking glances his way. Rebar responded with smiles. He thought he might have more luck here than in that Denver bar. Finally, the receptionist went into the conference room. "Sheriff, you've got to see her – she's driving me nuts."

"That's what I pay you for."

"It ain't enough."

"So get a job on a fishing boat."

The receptionist slammed the door shut as she went back to her desk. Rebar figured she must be one of the sheriff's relatives. Who else would have the nerve to talk to him that way?

Eventually, Sheriff Pickett gave in and went to the outer office to greet his visitors. "Why Mrs. Linn, what brings you here? I hope you haven't been waiting too long. Who is this young man you have with you today?"

"We both know you saw me pull into the parking space, and you know why I'm here, Sheriff. This is the witness to what you call the 'incident' that caused my son's death. His name is Reynold Barr. Your office was supposed to have him detained at the Cook County Jail, but as usual, you didn't follow through with it."

Sheriff Pickett reacted to this statement by raising his left eyebrow and grimacing, but said nothing to Jeanette Linn in response.

"I brought my own chair so let's get into your office and get started with you telling me about the investigation. Mr. Barr, please wheel me in."

"Of course, you know that you are welcome any time. My door is always open to any citizen."

Jeanette sighed and loudly cleared her throat. When Rebar was seated, she began. "Mr. Barr, please tell the sheriff what happened on the night in question."

Rebar launched into a ten minute monologue about the incident at Monty Tipsword's trailer. There was no way to interrupt him. He knew the details the way an actor knows his lines.

When Rebar finally finished, Sheriff Pickett shuffled a folder on his desk and pulled out a report. "This may seem off the subject, but Mrs. Linn, are you familiar with anyone from Arizona with the last name of Clements?"

"Yes, that's the last name of the brothers who robbed our pharmacy in Clarkwood. My son Todd's eyewitness testimony was what put them in jail."

"Well, one of my deputies found them lurking near your house a couple of days before Mr. Tipsword's party."

Jeanette looked completely shocked. It was apparent that she had not received the warning email that Mayor Cotton had promised Alex he would send her.

"When did they get out of prison? Why wasn't I notified? Why wasn't I told before now about them spying on Todd and me?"

"I don't know why nobody told you about the Clements brothers' release, but I didn't mention it before now because they didn't appear to have committed any crime. They said they were looking for their friend, Todd. Their story didn't quite ring true but, as I said, we had no reason to hold them. One of my deputies escorted them to the county line. We watched for them to see if they came back to Delmarva, but it doesn't appear that they ever did. However, if we are going to have a case that we can take to court and get a conviction, we'll surely have to follow up on this lead. Guess my chief deputy needs to take a little trip to Arizona."

"I've never told you how to investigate, Sheriff. Just do what you have to do."

"What about Mr. Barr's role in this?"

"I hired Mr. Alex Mann – you remember him don't you? – to track down Mr. Barr, since it appears you were lacking money or something to do it. Mr. Mann paid his bail in Denver and brought him here to me."

"He kidnapped Mr. Barr?"

"Not exactly, I had authorized Mr. Mann to offer to pay all of Mr. Barr's expenses to get here and to hire him as my caregiver. I'm paying him a salary about twice what Todd used to make fishing. I figured that would make him stay voluntarily. I'm upholding my part of the bargain. Right, Mr. Barr?"

"Yes, Ma'am and Sir, and so am I."

"What if I decide that he needs to be jailed as a material witness to keep him from running away?"

"The deal still holds. He gets twice the pay of a fisherman for sitting in jail and playing cards or whatever you have your prisoners do."

Sheriff Pickett had to think this over:

"Barr gets paid more than I do for sitting in my jail doing nothing. He gets free food, medical care if he needs it and can laugh at me all he wants. No way that I'm going to do that. He can at least empty her bedpan for his money. If he flees then, I have no worries, and there won't be any trial."

He turned to Jeanette, "Okay, we'll decide if we need to incarcerate Mr. Barr at a later date."

"You've been giving me the run around about my son's death ever since it happened. Now I'm going to make you a deal. You know that ever since we came to Delmarva and opened Linn's Float-a-Check business, we have been making loans to the citizens at rates well below the legal limit. Well, here is my deal. If you don't have a case ready to present to the district attorney by this date next month, I'm going to raise my interest rates to the legal limit. When people ask why the cost went up so much, I'll be only too happy to let them know that it was the only way that I could prod you into action. I'll stay away from any campaigning against you to avoid breaking any election laws. I'll just tell the truth and let the people decide." She scowled, and then said emphatically, "Take me to my car, Mr. Barr."

"Sounds more like a threat than a deal to me, Mrs. Linn." She ignored his comment and Rebar wheeled her out of the office. Sheriff Pickett became red in the face. He had swallowed his wad of chaw. After he stopped coughing and retching, he regained his breath and summoned his chief deputy. "We've got to get some action on that Toddler Linn death case or Old Lady Linn is going to have my job."

"How would she do that?"

"Says she's going to raise the interest rates on everyone's loans and tell them it's because I haven't brought anybody to trial in the death of her son."

Beads of sweat appeared on the forehead of the deputy. "How are we going to get rid of her?"

"Can't. The result would be the same. Some loan company would move in here and raise the interest rates to the legal limit anyhow. She'd have let everybody know beforehand, and then we would be under suspicion. Two wrongs ain't going to make this right."

"True."

"Looks like we're going to have to sacrifice Tipsword."

"Good idea. We'll make it look like she put out a contract on him, right?"

"What are you saying? I didn't mean it that way – just use him as a scapegoat."

"Maybe we don't have to do that. What about those kids that were driving around Old Lady Linn's house that night? Weren't they from Arkansas?"

"Arizona. Hey! Ain't that the place Linn's P.I. is from? Maybe there's some connection. Get a hold of the sheriff of that county and make arrangements to go see him. Run an NCIC check on those punks, too. Get out there, and I mean yesterday."

"Will do. But it'll be tomorrow before I can get there."

"Just get."

The next day Sheriff Pickett's Chief Deputy was westbound airborne. The flight would get into Phoenix late so he would have to stay overnight before meeting with the Yavanino County Sheriff.

"Those boys are the usual suspects in just about every crime in this part of the county, but I don't think they'd murder anybody."

"Well, I need to talk to them real bad."

"Okay. I'll have them picked up and brought here for questioning. They know the drill."

Maury Clements was brought into the interview room first. The Yavanino County Deputy read him his Miranda rights then left the room. The Challenger County Chief Deputy made it clear that he was operating under the same Miranda rights and began his questioning. "We think that you killed Todd Linn."

"Well, you think wrong."

"Why?"

"We couldn't find him."

"What do you mean?"

"We drove out there with our minds set on evening the score, but you don't have addresses, so we had a hard time tracking him down. We bought new rifles and sighted them and everything, but you found us before we found him. We decided that we'd be caught too easily after you got all of our contact information, so we just hustled back to Arizona. We wanted him dead but didn't we want to die ourselves."

No matter how the questions were phrased and repeated, Maury stuck to his story. After about an hour, Soger Clements was brought in, Mirandized, asked the same questions, gave the same answers and stuck to the story.

Frustrated, Challenger County's chief deputy gave up and returned home. He met with Sheriff Pickett the following afternoon.

"No luck with the Clements brothers. Why not just arrest that Barr guy and charge him?"

"First, we've got no proof. Second, we've got no evidence. Third, we've got no witnesses – remember that Monty never blamed the stranger – if he changed his story now it wouldn't look good. Fourth, I'm not allowing Old Lady Linn to pay that drifter more than I make to sit in my jail and eat the county's food."

"Then we got no choice but to hand over this case to the DA and ask her to charge Monty with Toddler's death."

"Let's get the paperwork ready."

Finally, eight months after the night of Monty Tipsword's infamous party, the murder of Todd Linn case was going to trial.

Sheriff Pickett and his deputy drove out to Monty's trailer the following evening, armed with the arrest warrant they received from the county district attorney. The court considered him to be a defendant with a very low risk of fleeing, so it allowed Monty to remain free until his upcoming trial. Rebar was an expected witness for the prosecution, so the sheriff hoped that the two men's paths didn't cross in the interim.

14

April 1, 1993
Tampa Bay, Florida

Alex Mann's thirst for knowledge led him to attend frequent pharmacy-related continuing education classes and seminars. Since his pharmacy school days, he had been particularly interested in learning more about the drug, warfarin. Alex had been eager to hear a presentation on warfarin from Dr. Herman Heller, a world-renowned expert on the drug. He was stocky, with Freud-like facial features, and he perpetually maintained an unlit cigar between the index and middle fingers of his left hand. The famed scientist conducted his research in San Francisco and was well-known for his entertaining and absorbing lectures.

Shortly after the packed seminar audience was seated, Dr. Heller gave a lively, animated seventy-minute retrospective of warfarin. He further engaged the audience by springing about to ever-changing empty seats in the conference room to make direct eye contact with nearby conferees.

"To begin, thank you all for coming. If you are here to listen to a God's-honest, entirely factual account of the evolution of warfarin from, as we say, 'silo to hypo,' then I'll most likely disappoint you. There were so many holes remaining in the drug's historical progression that I took the liberty of including certain 'what ifs' to fill-in some of those holes. Now with that disclaimer, my dear friends, I will begin.

1921 was not a good year for many upper Midwest dairy farmers. They had been hit hard financially – beaten down by severe weather, dicey grazing conditions, poor milk prices and broken farm equipment. The farmers finally thought they had caught a lucky break when they were approached by grain and feed salesmen who told them they could supply them with sweet clover hay at half the price of alfalfa hay. Many of the farmers reasoned that cows often free graze on sweet clover without mishap, so they couldn't see why they shouldn't buy the sweet clover to use for fodder fermented in a silo, called 'silage.'

A few weeks later, many were devastated when they saw their prized Guernseys, as well as their livelihoods suddenly perish due to an unknown cattle disease.

They had heard that farmers all over the northern United States and Canada had their cattle hemorrhaging and internally bleeding to death in sizeable numbers. Later that year, a Canadian veterinary pathologist named Frank Schofield, while researching the disease, discovered that the cattle eating sweet clover silage were the ones that contracted the malady. Dr. Schofield found that silage made from sweet clover functioned as a powerful anticoagulant. Only silage made from sweet clover caused the disease.

When the sweet clover hay is converted to silage, instead of improving its nutritional value as it does with alfalfa, it produced a substance that inhibits the body's production of Vitamin K. When the body does not have enough Vitamin K, it loses the ability to clot blood. Dr. Karl Paul Link at the University of Wisconsin manipulated the disease-causing molecule and called the substance 'warfarin.' It was initially introduced in 1948 as a pesticide against rats and mice."

Dr. Heller paused for a few moments to gauge his audience's interest level. Noticing that they were awake, he continued. "In 1951, a U.S. military recruit unsuccessfully attempted to commit suicide by ingesting several doses of rodent killer containing warfarin. Apparently, he had decided he would rather kill himself in the United States, than be killed in combat in Korea. The medical staff treated him with the known specific antidote, vitamin K, and he fully recovered in the hospital.

Although in the early 1950's warfarin was found to be effective and relatively safe for preventing abnormal formation and migration of blood clots in many disorders, and was approved for use as a medication in 1954, the pharmacy standards then would have never met today's rigorous requirements. Interest in the use of warfarin as a therapeutic anticoagulant had just begun, and it would be years before anecdotal data on which to base conclusions would be available.

To test a new drug in the mid-1950s, doctors were given free samples, and told to give them to their patients. If a patient had an adverse reaction to the medication, the doctors were to notify the drug companies to tell them about the patient's medical issues. Taking more warfarin than was needed caused the blood to fail to clot. This led doctors to conclude that a patient's blood was too thin, and warfarin became known as a blood thinner. This outdated concept remains, despite the fact that today's technology shows that taking warfarin does not change the blood's viscosity."

Dr. Heller paused again. Before continuing his talk, he poured himself a glass of ice water from the pitcher on the table next to this lectern, took a few sips, checked his watch and found another empty seat in the audience.

Alex Mann had a long-time fascination with the evolution of drug dosing. He was especially interested in seeing how many improper dosing incidents were tied in with crimes. Alex ascribed to the notion that what outwardly may seem like an unfortunate negative reaction to a type or dosage of a medication may be something more sinister. He recognized and applauded the strides that the medical field and pharmaceutical companies had made with proper dosing, yet contended that a certain number of pharmacological-related deaths were of questionable causes.

Dr. Heller continued his address to the conferees. "Here come the good parts," he said with an exaggerated wink. Warfarin gained both acclaim and notoriety in its history. In September 1955, U.S. President Dwight D. Eisenhower became an early recipient of warfarin after suddenly suffering a heart attack in Colorado, and was rushed to Fitzsimons Army Hospital in Denver for treatment.

Once the news hit the press, it caused a brief panic on Wall Street. It was the first, and so far the only time a president had suffered a heart attack while in office, and the nation was nervous and distraught. After seven weeks, the nation's leader recovered and was allowed to return to Washington, D.C. and to a relieved public.

At Walter Reid Army Hospital, where Eisenhower's recovery continued, it was the highlight of one radiologist's career when he was ordered to do total body x-rays on the ailing president. The commander-and-chief's entourage, including secret service agents, the chief of radiology, the commanding general at the hospital, and even Mamie Eisenhower, hovered over the young doctor, to make certain that every setting was correct.

'You never forget something like that,' the now retired radiologist told me when we met years later at a medical convention. 'Think about it,' he said. 'We were only one heartbeat away from having Richard Nixon as our president thirteen years earlier than expected.'"

Many members of the audience tittered at that remark. Dr. Heller smiled, and then found a new seat, first row center – his back to the conferees – and continued. "On the flip side, Joseph Stalin, the notorious former leader of the Soviet Union died from a brain hemorrhage at his home in 1953. Many in Stalin's 'inner circle' felt that his provocative and aggressive manner in dealing with Soviet citizens and the other nations' leaders spelled world-wide disaster. Stalin was known to be extremely paranoid, and was intent on killing anyone whom he perceived was out to destroy him.

Nikolai Alistratov was a laborer who lived in a poor section of Moscow in 1953 and who had the dubious honor of being selected as one of a group of Muscovites to be invited to a fine dinner at Premier Stalin's Kremlin palace.

The special dinner invitation had no RSVP. Attendance was mandatory, and was presented as an opportunity for common citizens to sample the dinner recipes that would later be served to Stalin after they ate.

In reality, it was Stalin's fear of being poisoned that lead him to use human guinea pigs to eat the same food he would eat once he made sure that nobody got sick and died from that meal's cuisine. Stalin assumed that all poisons were very fast-acting, and the consequences of ingesting them would be immediately evident. Normally, a person would serve as a 'taster' only once or twice, but while driving through the common streets outside the Kremlin, the lead car of Stalin's motorcade had struck and killed Nikolai's dog. In an uncharacteristic gesture of compassion, Stalin had Nikolai informed that he was to be compensated for the loss of his beloved pet by attending one full week of meals at Stalin's palace. Neighbors joked that he was Stalin's new best friend. Nikolai wondered how he should feel about such a 'gift,' but as no one had shown any signs of poisoning after eating the meals, Nikolai and Stalin continued to eat confidently, and with gusto.

Unexpectedly, on February 26, after his sixth day of dining at the Kremlin, Nikolai went home and collapsed on his kitchen floor. Blood was surging from his nose and ears, and he thrashed his body uncontrollably. With no medical care or friends to look in on him, he died a painful death. Two Kremlin Guards showed up at Nikolai's house late the next afternoon to demand that he tell them why he was not present for Soviet Premier Stalin's meals.

One guard gasped when he first saw the body on the floor while the other guard kicked at it to see if he was drunk or dead. When questioned, the guards told Stalin's chief of staff that Nikolai Alistratov had died of what looked like natural causes. The Kremlin doctors had no intention of performing an autopsy on him, so his body had been quickly cremated,

A few days later, Joseph Stalin met a similar fate. On March 1, 1953, after his final dinner with four trusted members of his Politburo, Stalin suffered extensive stomach hemorrhaging as he writhed in agony. His Politburo colleagues refused to get him medical help in the first hours of his illness when it might have been effective. They allegedly thought he had drunk too much and fell out of bed. Stalin died four days later at age seventy-three. The official cause of death was a hemorrhage on the left side of his brain.

Some doctors remain skeptical that a conclusive answer to the qucstion of whether or not he was poisoned will ever be found, even if an autopsy was performed today with all of the latest technology. Even now, some still believe that Stalin was poisoned by his doctors who were allied with a group driven by fear of a nuclear holocaust and the desire to avert a possible war with the United States.

His doctors' descriptions of Stalin's behavior and ailments during his last days suggest that he may havc bcen poisoned with warfarin, which was used at that time as a rodent killer. Many physicians who reviewed the Soviet doctors' official report of Stalin's final days concluded that similar physical effects could have been produced by a five-to-ten-day overdose of that drug. Oh – and in case you're wondering, to my knowledge, nothing more has ever been learned about the untimely and unexplained death of the 'taster,' Nikolai Alistratov."

Alex was enraptured with Dr. Heller's warfarin presentation. After it concluded, several attendees, including Alex, approached the famed expert, heaping him with praises.

After the crowd died down, Alex took the liberty of following Dr. Heller out to his late model silver Audi sedan. They talked for only a few minutes, and exchanged business cards before departing. Alex left with a standing invitation from Dr. Heller to call him if he ever needed his assistance. At that moment, neither man could have realized the significance of their next encounter.

15

Tuesday, March 20, 2001
Delmarva

Three weeks before Monty Tipsword's April 9 trial for murdering Todd Linn was to begin, Alex Mann scheduled a brief meeting with the defense attorney, Farleigh Mullanphy. Mr. Mullanphy was not only surprised, but wary about taking the meeting. He understood that Alex worked for Jeanette Linn and the prosecution. During their meeting, Alex repeated to Farleigh what he had said to Jeanette Linn, "The best investigators follow the clues wherever they lead."

In Alex's opinion, due to a lack of evidence, proving that Monty was guilty of second degree murder was not going to be easy for the prosecutor. Given Todd's serious medical problems, Alex had begun to explore the possibility that there may have been extenuating circumstances that contributed to Todd's death. He told Farleigh that the case was more than simply deciding between the two options of "was he pushed?" or "did he accidentally fall?"

Farleigh Mullanphy stared straight at Alex and said, "I've got three questions for you:

A – Does Judge Barton know you're talking to me?

B – Does Prosecutor Meade know we're talking? and

C – Tell me again why you're doing this?"

"Right now I'm not on either side. I'm also not a witness for the prosecution. I told you that I go where the evidence leads me. I want to know the truth about how Todd died as much as Jeanette Linn or you, or anyone."

"I see, but you didn't answer my first two questions, and I just thought of a fourth one: Does Jeanette Linn know you're here?"

Alex hesitated a moment, then replied, "No" – "no" – and "no" to your questions. Why? – could we get in trouble for having this conversation?"

Farleigh stood abruptly and growled, "*We*? Are *we* in trouble?"

"Look," Alex countered, "I don't intend on giving you any confidential information. I'm only making a suggestion that you contact Dr. Herman Heller. He works out of San Francisco but travels a great deal. He's an internationally-known expert on the drug, warfarin. I think he would make an excellent expert witness for the defense."

"How so?"

"Dr. Heller may be able to add credence to a theory which suggests that there is an alternative medical explanation for Todd Linn's death, and it includes the negative effects of taking warfarin. His research and expert testimony in past criminal cases is likely to at least create reasonable doubt in the jurors' minds about whether or not Monty intentionally killed Todd. Or for that matter, if he had anything to do with causing Todd's death. Believe me, those are questions I've been struggling unsuccessfully to answer. I don't think we'll ever know what was on Monty's mind that night Todd fell down those stairs."

"And you think the testimony of a drug specialist is going to help Monty beat a 'Murder 2' rap?"

"I believe in the integrity of Dr. Heller's research. You owe it to your client to at least hear what he has to say."

"Sounds to me like you've switched sides and have gotten on the Monty bandwagon."

"I've already told you that's not why I'm here. If I never find out 'why' Todd Linn died, I'd at least like to know 'how' he died. I doubt that Monty will be confessing to anything, anytime soon."

"We go to trial early next month. Do you know if this Dr. Heller is available on April 9? Do you know if he would be on-board with testifying as our expert witness?"

Alex leaned forward in his seat and mimicked Farleigh Mullanphy muffled growl, "*Our*? *Our* expert witness?"

"I meant my defense team – not you – remember, you aren't an *our*."

"Dr. Heller is a professional acquaintance of mine. I took the liberty of calling him about the case. He said he would be very willing to talk with you. Oh, and he is available on the 9th.

16

Sunday, April 8, 2001
Delmarva

The day before the Monty Tipsword trial, Winnie called Alex to wish him luck in finding the truth about Todd Linn's death. She had originally intended on being in court, but the Colorado Pharmacy Board had just lowered the boom on Winnie. They suspended her without pay, pending the outcome of their internal investigation of her performance and conduct. She figured that the news of her suspension had already hit the law enforcement wires and that showing up at trial was not in anyone's best interest.

"Alex, it's Winnie."

"Win-Win, what's the situation?"

"Likely unemployment. I'm pretty sure I'm about to get canned."

"Oh no! I guess your threats to expose the agency didn't help after all. I'm sorry – I feel responsible."

"Don't blame yourself, Alex. It was my choice, and I actually had a blast helping you with the investigation. I can't work for an employer that's constantly looking over my shoulder. I know that I bent the rules – well, and the law – several times, but it was all for a noble purpose."

"Winnie, you'll always be a winner. When this trial is over, we can figure what you can do next. I still have other job connections."

"Thanks, Alex. Just as long as I don't end up a winner in prison stripes."

"I'll call you after the trial and let you know all the details. Let's get together when things are resolved with you at work. Remember, I owe you a bowl or two of pho. Oh – and Winnie, I hope we can work together again."

Winnie began to tear up ever so slightly and said, "You can count on it, Alex," and she meant it.

17

Monday, April 9 - Wednesday, April 11, 2001
Delmarva

"Oyez! Oyez! Oyez!" cried the Clerk of the Superior Court of Challenger County at precisely ten o'clock in the morning. "All rise. The Honorable Judge Noble Barton is presiding."

In strode the judge. Her curly snow-white hair was almost a caricature of a British barrister's powdered wig and made an appropriate topping for her flowing black robe.

"You may be seated," said the court clerk. Everyone sat except Judge Barton who had an odd habit of pacing back-and-forth behind the bench and occasionally around the perimeter of the courtroom. She was not a member of the usual panel of judges who heard cases in Challenger County.

Judge Barton had been brought in for this case from the farthest district in the state. Challenger County had among the lowest per capita income in the state and was also one of the least populated. They rarely had a court case with such a serious charge as second-degree murder.

Since the county could ill afford the expense of transporting the lawyers, jury members and witnesses to a different venue, it was common practice in serious cases for the opposing attorneys to agree to have only a presiding judge brought in from a distant jurisdiction. While this offended the sensibilities of attorneys from *away*, it was how things were in this small, poor, exceedingly rural county.

"The Superior Court of Challenger County will now consider case 990014 known as 'The People v. Monty Tipsword'." called the Clerk of the Court in a voice that was too loud and designed to impress his importance to others.

"Let the record show that the people are represented by counsel Dana Meade in her capacity as District Attorney and the defendant, Monty Tipsword, represented by counsel, Farleigh Mullanphy, began Judge Barton. "Are the attorneys ready to initiate jury selection?" she asked.

"Yes, Your Honor," both attorneys replied.

"Bailiff, please bring in the first twenty potential jurors and have them seated," Judge Barton ordered.

The bailiff led twenty Delmarva citizens, dressed in their Sunday best, into the courtroom.

The judge began her usual spiel for a panel of jurors. "I want you to know that jury duty is a serious civic duty, not to be taken lightly. In this court, it is my duty to determine what the law states. It is thc jury's duty to listen to testimony and determine what the truth is. You will hear at least two sides to every story and probably many more versions of what people thought they saw and heard. Using only testimony that is admissible in this court, your duty is to determine what is most likely the truth. The court expects you to take this duty very seriously. You should not attempt to evade, that means get out of, jury duty unless it will place a serious hardship on you, or you have a legitimate conflict of interest. The attorneys for each side may preemptively, that means that no reason need be given, reject as many as five potential jurors.

This does not reflect in any way on your character. It may be as simple as they do not want you on the jury because your spouse is related to one of the parties involved."

There was an instant outbreak of throat-clearing and feet-shuffling by the spectators in the courtroom in anticipation of what was about to happen. Judge Barton gave the courtroom a stern look but was clueless as to what caused the outburst. Continuing, she asked Potential Juror Number One to stand and state her name.

"Jennifer Tipsword," Potential Juror Number One stated.

"Are you in any way related to the defendant?" Judge Barton asked.

"Your Honor, my husband and Monty are cousins," she replied.

"You are dismissed," Judge Barton stated. This brought on a wave of head-shaking and murmuring in the courtroom. It was quickly subdued by a menacing glare from the judge.

"Potential Juror Number Two please stand and state your name," Judge Barton continued.

"Roger Tipsword."

"Are you…"

"Yes, Your Honor, Monty's Pa and I are brothers."

"You are dismissed," Judge Barton again stated.

"Potential Juror Number Three please rise and state your name," ordered Judge Barton.

"Amanda Tipsword."

"And how are you related?"

"Me and Monty are cousins. His mother and my father are sister and brother."

"Bailiff!" Judge Barton called out, "Are you sure that there has been no monkey business in the selection of these potential jurors. Can you guarantee me that they were randomly selected?"

"Yes, Your Honor."

"Alright then let us proceed. Potential Juror Number Four, are you also a Tipsword?" Judge Barton asked.

"No, Your Honor. I'm an *away*."

"What do you mean by that?"

"Well that's what they call us people here who weren't born in Challenger County."

Judge Barton asked, "Who are 'they'?

"They that were born in Challenger County."

"Good, maybe we are making some progress, then," responded the judge.

This brought an outburst of laughter from the spectators and potential jurors alike and received a rebuking frown from the bench.

"Please state your name."

"Beth Pickett, and before you ask, Your Honor, my husband is the sheriff's brother."

Judge Barton now realized that she was the only one in the courtroom who did not understand the make up of the population of Challenger County.

"Bailiff, have the potential jurors leave the courtroom subject to my recalling them."

"Yes, Your Honor. Jurors, please leave the courtroom and meet in the jury room in five minutes," he instructed.

"Counsel for both sides approach the bench," Judge Barton ordered. She stopped her pacing and joined them.

"Obviously you both knew what was happening but did not inform me in advance of this unusual set of circumstances. It is also obvious that you have dealt with this situation previously, so now please tell the court how you intend to deal with all of these relatives being potential jurors. Prosecution, you go first."

"Your Honor it all started back in 1670."

"We have to discuss over four hundred years of history?" Judge Barton exclaimed.

"Yes, Your Honor, we do if the court wishes to really understand what is happening."

"Proceed."

"In 1670, about fifty years after the "Mayflower" landed, the "St. Anne" was bound for Plymouth Colony when a northeaster pushed her south, and she grounded on this remote swamp. Almost half the people on the ship were Tipswords and the other half were Picketts and Meades. For about twenty years, nobody knew that the survivors were here. By that time, many of the original party were dead, and this area had become home to the second generation. They were finally discovered by neighboring colonies but refused all offers of rescue.

They set up a justice system but had to rely on folks being honest when they had to testify for or against their kin. The court had to adapt to this unusual population, and they've been doing so ever since. And, Your Honor, if I could interject my opinion, I'd be willing to bet that our witnesses tell the truth more often than in any other court in the country. We pretty well know who did what to whom."

"Okay, but defense, do you agree to this?"

"We do, Your Honor. As counsel stated it's a time-honored tradition. As we see it, the court action only makes it official."

"Alright, since this seems to work, bailiff, recall the potential jurors."

The seventeen remaining jury candidates smiled proudly as they marched back into the courtroom; confident that their officials had hashed things out with the judge and let her know how life was in their world.

Judge Barton resumed the proceedings. "Let the records show that the prosecution and counsel for the defense have both agreed that it is common practice in this jurisdiction to allow persons related to principals in the case to be members of the jury. Henceforth, the bench will not automatically issue dismissal notices for potential jurors based on relationships to any party in the case."

Over the next two hours, the jury selection continued about as smoothly as could be expected. The prosecution preemptively dismissed Gloria Tipsword-Acorn, the defendant's sister while the prosecution used its prerogative to dismiss the sheriff's wife. It wasn't because they thought that Mrs. Pickett was prejudiced. Rather, they acknowledged that if she were on the jury, there wouldn't be anyone who could fix food for everyone. As the Challenger County residents put it, "We wouldn't get mutton."

After six jurors were selected, Judge Barton summoned the attorneys for both sides to the bench. "Do you have any objections to breaking for lunch?" she asked.

"No, Your Honor," both replied simultaneously.

"How long is it customary to take?" queried Judge Barton.

"About ninety minutes. The bailiff has the sheriff's wife bring in sandwiches and cookies for the jurors and potential jurors. The rest of us are going across the street to 'The Charge'. That's what we call Pickett's Pub."

The judge looked at him blankly.

"Remember Pickett's Charge? The battle? By the way, they just take cash if you're an *away.* It's the only place in town that you can get mutton besides the Senior Center, and they want reservations twenty-four hours in advance. When we all get to Pickett's it will be too much for the one or two waitresses and one cook to get us out any quicker than ninety minutes."

"Court will recess for lunch," Judge Barton ordered. "It will reconvene promptly at two o'clock." She thought to herself that surely an hour and forty-five minutes would be sufficient for lunch in this little burg. She went to the judges' chamber and removed her robe, used the restroom, refreshed her make-up and "charged over" to Pickett's. That little delay in leaving assured her of being the last one into the establishment, and resulted in her finding only one empty seat in the house – a stool at the bar. The judge's lunch order sat at the bottom of a huge stack of orders already waiting to be filled.

It was seven minutes to two o'clock when her plate finally arrived. As she swallowed her soft-shell crab sandwich with a minimum of chewing, the honorable judge resolved to pick up something for lunch at the convenience store in the morning before the next court session.

"All rise, the court is back in session," cried the clerk at two-fifteen as Judge Noble Barton strode into the courtroom and paced behind the bench. She looked slightly irritated, and a little flustered by the lunchtime rat-race at The Charge, but managed to maintain her dignity.

"Let us resume jury selection," she ordered. It took less than an hour to finish the process.

"Would both sets of attorneys approach the bench?" Judge Barton phrased her order in the form of a question. "I see no reason why we couldn't continue until five o'clock. Does either side have any objection?"

"We have a problem, Your Honor," stated the prosecuting attorney. We had instructed the first witnesses to be available at two o'clock this afternoon. Two of them are in the waiting area, but the person we had planned to call first is not present."

"Who is this person?" asked the judge.

"Juanda Tipsword. She is to be the one to place both the accused and the deceased simultaneously at the scene of the incident."

"That seems a reasonable place to start," commented the judge. "By the way, what is her relationship to the accused?"

"She is the cousin of the accused and was also the girlfriend of the deceased."

Judge Barton loudly cleared her throat.

"Your Honor," the prosecutor hastily added.

"Bailiff, have you seen Juanda Tipsword today?"

"No, Your Honor."

"Is the sheriff available to go look for her?"

"I believe so, Your Honor. You want me to get him?"

The bailiff stepped into the hall and called out, "Sheriff, the judge wants you."

The sheriff hauled his considerable bulk up off a bench, expectorated a sizeable wad of chewed tobacco into the pot of an artificial palm tree, and waddled into the court room.

"Sheriff Pickett, could you locate Juanda Tipsword for the court?"

In hopes of avoiding close scrutiny from the bench, he played up his role as just a good old country boy. "I allowed that you were going to ask that Your Honor, ma'am, so I've been looking into the matter since finishing my mutton. Nobody has seen 'fidney bits' of her since about seven o'clock last night when she drove south out of town. I just came back from her trailer five minutes ago, but I can go back in a 'whipstitch' if it would please Your Honor."

"No, I guess that will not be necessary. It's getting late, so I believe that we will just adjourn until tomorrow morning. Members of the Jury, I understand that it is extremely likely that you have all heard opinions of this case. However, the standard procedure for courts in this state is for the judge to order that you not discuss this case with anyone outside the courtroom or the jury room while the case is being tried. You are not to watch the TV news or listen to the radio news, or read the newspaper or even use a computer to gain any information about this case.

If anyone approaches you to mention this case for any reason you are to notify the bailiff before court resumes in the morning. If you accidentally overhear anything to do with this case, report it to the bailiff. If it was accidental, you will not be held in contempt of court. However, if you willfully discuss the case or do not report anything that could affect your opinion of the case you will likely be held in contempt of court. Court will reconvene promptly at nine o'clock tomorrow morning. Bailiff, please give the jury instructions so that they will be ready. We trust that Juanda Tipsword and all other necessary witnesses will be here tomorrow and on time. Court is recessed until nine o'clock."

Granny Pickett ran the only bed and breakfast in Delmarva. Judge Barton had obtained a room with a nice view of the water – not really a difficult feat since she and Alex Mann were the only guests. This morning at breakfast the ninety-six year old Granny "allowed as how she was feeling puny," but still offered to fix a dinner for the judge. Judge Barton declined but asked where she might go for dinner. Granny explained how to find The Crab Palace in the town of Dollar's Quarter (or "Two Bits" as it was called locally). Since there was only one paved road out of Delmarva and that The Crab Palace in Two Bits was on that road, Granny told her honor that she couldn't miss them.

Noble Barton set out for The Crab Palace in Two Bits as soon as court was recessed. During the entire seventeen-mile drive, the only other vehicle she noticed was a battered, ancient, red pickup truck stopped and blocking the opposite lane.

Once she reached The Crab Palace, Judge Barton let out a gasp – "palace" was a gross misnomer.

She didn't know whether the owner had failed to reach his goal or had a sick sense of humor.

"Evening, Your Honor," the effervescent young waitress greeted her. She was a spittin' image of the B&B owner, and the judge more than suspected that she was probably Granny's great-granddaughter, and that Granny had tipped her off.

"Sit anywhere Your Honor likes."

Judge Barton looked around and picked the only booth that was lacking a duct tape patch. When she was seated, she looked at the ceiling and noticed a large drop of grease hanging from the air duct directly above her table. She considered moving but reasoned that it had probably been threatening to drop since the ill-fated flight of the Hindenburg blimp, so she settled in.

The waitress brought a red plastic glass of water and asked, "What would you like, Dea… I mean Your Honor?"

"What's the best thing you have?"

"Deviled crab cakes with spar-grass casserole."

"Is spar-grass like asparagus?"

"Well, I think spar-grass is what *aways* call asparagus. But I got to warn Your Honor – it takes a mite to fix so don't order that if Your Honor is flummoxed for time."

"I think that 'time' is the one thing I have plenty of this evening, so I'll follow your meal suggestion."

Fortunately, the honorable judge had a few easy-reading books in her bag. In due time, the order arrived. The food was delicious – homemade comfort food really. Judge Barton settled her bill and headed out to her car.

Before the judge even left the parking lot, the helpful waitress was on the phone. "Granny, she left me a five dollar tip. Can you imagine that? Five bucks for one person in this two-bit town!"

Judge Barton drove carefully back to Delmarva. She was correct in surmising that the broken-down truck was probably still on the road, only this time there was a flurry of activity around it.

She made her way back to Granny's B&B and was greeted at the door by Granny herself. "Did you find The Crab Palace, sure enough?"

"Sure enough," replied the judge.

"How was the food?"

"Great – it was like I was eating in a friend's kitchen."

"I'm sure they enjoyed having you there," Granny said with a smile. "What time would you like breakfast in the morning? I'll make my breakfast casserole."

"Seven will be perfect for me, is that okay for you?"

"Perfect for me, too. Have a nice sleep."

At seven o'clock sharp, Judge Nobel Barton walked downstairs to the dining room. She had been awakened an hour earlier by the delicious smell of frying pork sausage for Granny's breakfast casserole. Granny offered to pack up some of the leftovers for the judge's lunch, but thinking that she should have a less fattening meal, Judge Barton declined. She intended to get some fruit at the convenience store for lunch instead. She did take Granny up on her offer of fixing dinner that evening.

Minutes later, the judge arrived at Swigs Liquors, Delmarva's only convenience store and was greeted by an astonishing array of offerings. Judge Barton was so surprised that she began to count the selections. There were forty-six different facings of beer when you counted the various brands, bottle sizes, can sizes, and whether they were singles, six-packs, twelve-packs or twenty-four-packs. Next came the twenty-one facings of whiskey. There were no other forms of alcohol on display. There were thirty-seven types of soft drinks – all with sugar – nobody around here wasted money on fake soda. There was one quart bottle of milk available, and it had an expiration date that coincided with that day's date. Next were ninety-eight facings of salty snacks, exceeded only by the one hundred-two facings of candy bars. There were also thirty-six facings of Spam®.

No fruit seemed to be available – not even canned fruit – so the judge began looking for a sandwich. There was one in the refrigerator case – baloney laced with olives and pimentos. When the judge commented on the limited selection, the elderly clerk replied from her perch, "Yeah, Mutton Man ain't been by in more than a week." Judge Barton proceeded to the courthouse empty-handed and locked herself in the judge's chamber.

She wanted to cry, but it didn't seem right to cry for her own situation. She would be out of here before the end of the week. She considered crying for the people stuck in this existence, but they didn't seem particularly anxious to be "saved." She just sat with her head in her hands.

Meanwhile, people were gathering for the trial – spectators, witnesses, attorneys, paralegals, court reporters, jurors, and the expert witness for the defense, Herman Heller. As he reached the metal detector, Dr. Heller asked the guard if she had seen the defense attorney, Farleigh Mullanphy. She told him that she thought he had gone to the second floor. Unsuccessful in finding him there, Dr. Heller went back downstairs to the metal detector guard and asked if someone could help him locate the lead defense attorney.

The guard replied, "I'll go look for him but you have to stand here and not let anyone get by until I get back."

Dr. Heller was astounded by this command. He was now the acting gatekeeper for the courthouse security. He dutifully stood at his post for a couple of minutes until the guard returned with the sought-after Mr. Mullanphy. After each had introduced himself, the attorney told the doctor that he would probably not call him to the stand until after the lunch recess. Dr. Heller and his wife had combined a little vacation with his expert witness work, so she had dropped him off at the courthouse and immediately returned to the beach house they had rented about twenty-five miles away. The only option open to Dr. Heller was to watch the court proceedings until he was called, so he went back upstairs and took a seat outside the courtroom.

He realized that most of the characters he had spent hours studying in the reports for his expert opinion had suddenly come to life right in front of him. He began playing a game of guessing who was who. Dr. Heller was surprised when he learned that the man chatting nonchalantly with the crowd of observers was the defendant, Monty Tipsword, who had arrived at the trial unchaperoned by law enforcement.

Suddenly, as if a hurricane had blown in, everyone disappeared into the courtroom. There was no further entertainment to be had by sitting outside the courtroom, so Dr. Heller ventured in.

"Oyez! Oyez! Oyez!" cried the Clerk of the Superior Court of Challenger County at precisely nine o'clock in the morning. "All rise. The Honorable Judge Noble Barton is presiding."

In strode Judge Barton, but once again she did not take a seat on the bench. "You may be seated," called the clerk hoping that this time the judge heard him and would take her seat. But it was not to be. Everyone else heard and complied.

"Before the jury comes in, I would like to know if Juanda Tipsword is in the courtroom," Judge Barton rumbled in her most severe voice.

A heavyset young woman wearing a gown that would have been more appropriate for a nightclub than a courtroom stood and said, "I am, Your Honor."

"Ms. Tipsword, would you please come forward and have a seat on the witness stand?" Battling the long dress and high heels, Tipsy made her way forward.

"Ms. Tipsword, your absence from the courtroom yesterday has tempted me to cite you for contempt…"

Juanda did not let Judge Barton finish her sentence.

"Your Honor, it wasn't contempt for the court that caused me not to be here yesterday, but respect for the court. I'm all confused about what I am supposed to be feeling. I grew up with Monty. He's my cousin and just two weeks older than me. We've lived across the road door from each other all our lives. Sure he teased and pestered me as kids, but I don't want him to go to jail. But Todd was my boyfriend – not just my boyfriend, but the only guy who ever treated me right. He didn't care if I was just short of the size of a baby whale because he was powerfully big too. Now he's dead, and some think Monty killed him." She paused and took a deep breath. "I don't know what the truth is, but I decided that whatever the court decides will be the truth and I'll live with it. You look around this town, and you can see there ain't any cash money available. Have you had a reason to go into Swigs yet? There ain't enough honest-to-goodness, real food in there to keep two hummingbirds and a chipmunk fed. Why not? Because nobody's got any money. Everybody gets something and tells Swigs to 'jot it down.' Well the mutton man won't even come any more because he wants cash, not a bad check or anything else. Except for working for the 'gummint,' the only way you get cash money is working on a fishing boat. And then you got to be standing right next to Cap'n when he gets paid for the catch or he'll have it spent paying every other creature that's got a hand stuck out. So even though it ain't a place for a girl, Monty got me started at fishing."

"Please…" Judge Barton tried to interrupt.

"Your Honor, please hear me out. You talked about contempt so let me have my day in court."

Judge Barton was so stunned that for the first time in the two days of the trial that she actually took a seat on the bench.

"You ask anyone around here if they ever see me wearing anything but smelly fishing overalls. Well, I got up yesterday and went to put on my good pants to show respect for the court, and they didn't fit any more. Why, I would've had to sew a gusset in them to get them on. So I scraped together my money and what little my Mom could let me have, and I headed over to Two Bits to get something respectable that fit. Well, guess what, the only thing I could afford was this fifty percent marked down prom dress. This thing ain't no thicker than a 'skeeter's' wing, but it's more respectable than anything else I've got. I lit out of there for home in plenty of time to get to court by two o'clock, but then I punched a 'tar.'"

"You what?" asked the Honorable Judge.

"You know, I must've run over something that punched a hole in my 'tar' and it let all the air out. Well, I ain't got any money left at that point. I didn't even have enough to pay the tax on the dress. I walked home, and Monty helped me find a used 'tar' and put it on. By then it was dark. So as you can plainly see, Your Honor, I was trying to show respect for the court, not contempt. I've got nothing else to say." Juanda started to sob.

"Allow me to ask you one question," Judge Barton replied. "Was that your truck I saw on the side of the road last night when I was on my way to and returning from Dollar's Quarter?"

"Calling that contemptible critter a truck is giving it more respect than it's owed," Juanda replied. "But I guess it was."

The honorable judge thought:

"Lord have mercy on my soul, I'm starting to understand this place."

"Ms. Tipsword, I have never allowed such an outburst in my courtroom in twenty-six years on the bench, but I also doubt that I have ever heard anyone, even if they were sworn to tell the truth, make a more honest statement. You may have a seat in the waiting area. Please do not leave the courthouse. We don't want to have another punched tire hold us up."

"You don't need to worry about that, Your Honor. I walked over here today." Juanda exited the courtroom.

Judge Barton resumed her journey around the courtroom. "Bailiff, bring in the jurors," she ordered as she paced behind the bench.

Again the jurors shuffled into the courtroom and took their seats in the jury box.

"Clerk, administer the oath to the jurors."

When the jurors had been duly sworn, Judge Barton stopped her pacing and stood in front of the jury box. "I just want to remind you that you are to make your decision as to the guilt or innocence of the accused only on the basis of evidence that I allow to be presented to the court. What you think you know or feel you know or have heard about this case is not evidence. I want each of you to look me in the eye and answer that you understand."

As the judge stepped in front of the jurors, each responded with, "Yes, Your Honor." There were some who made only scanty eye contact, preferring to hang their heads instead.

Both sides made brief opening statements, which seemed mostly unnecessary to the jurors and spectators because everyone already knew why they were here.

"Prosecution, call your first witness."

"The prosecution summons Juanda Tipsword."

Juanda made her way to the witness stand and was sworn in.

County prosecutor Dana Meade stepped to within a few feet of the witness stand. She was an attractive woman in her late thirties, with pinned-up red hair and dressed all in black except, for a little patch of white blouse showing about her neckline. "Ms. Tipsword," she began, "on the night of July 21, 2000, there was a party at the home of your cousin, Monty Tipsword. Is that correct?"

"Yes."

"Do you know for a fact that Monty Tipsword was there?"

"Yes."

"Were you there?"

"No."

"Where were you?"

"I was at home."

"If you were at home, how do you know that Mr. Tipsword was there?"

"I live in the trailer across from his. I can see it real easy."

"What time did you see Mr. Tipsword at the trailer?"

"At nine o'clock."

"How do you know the exact time?"

"I turned off my TV when one of my favorite shows ended. I kinda wanted to keep an eye on what was going on."

"What did you think might happen?"

"Well, I thought Todd Linn might be there too."

"Was he there?"

"Yes."

"How could you see clearly if it was after nine o'clock?"

"I turned off my lights and opened my curtains."

"Was there enough light to see by?"

"Yes, Monty had his lights on."

"How sure are you that it was Mr. Tipsword and Mr. Linn that you saw?"

"Well, Monty is my cousin, and we have lived near each other almost all of our lives, so I know that it was him. And Todd was my boyfriend. There ain't nobody else around here that was anywhere near his size."

"How big was Mr. Linn?"

"About six feet eight, and over three hundred and fifty pounds."

"If your cousin and boyfriend were both there, why did you choose not to go along?"

"I thought something bad might happen."

"Like what?"

"That after they got drunk, Monty and Todd might fight."

"Why would they do that?"

"On the Tuesday before the party, Monty, Todd and I were working on the same boat. When we were hauling in our catch, Todd got his net tangled on a peg and nearly broke his wrist. He yelled for Monty to help him, but if Monty had, he would've dropped his side of the net and the catch would've been lost. I had to run over and help Todd get loose. There were a lot of angry words and name calling, but if they would've punched each other, Cap'n Miles would've docked both of them part of their share of the money. I was afraid things would boil over after they got a six-pack or two in them. I didn't want to see either one hurt, so I didn't go."

"Did they fight?"

"I didn't see any fighting."

"Did you recognize anyone else at the party?"

"The usual ones who want to bring a six-pack and drink twelve." Juanda Tipsword glanced around the courtroom.

"Was there anyone that you saw but did not recognize?"

"Yeah, I mean yes, there was a guy who looked a lot like Monty, but he walked different. Sort of rolled from side to side with each step. Nobody I know is that same size and walks like that."

"Did you sit there and watch all night?"

"No, I turned on Letterman, but they had a guest host I don't like, and I fell asleep."

"When did you wake up?"

"I don't remember exactly, but it was probably a little before midnight."

"Did you look out at the party?"

"Yeah, I mean yes."

"What did you see?"

"The party had broken up, but I saw a heap in the pile of wood chips at the bottom of the stairs of Monty's trailer."

"Could you describe the heap?"

"Well, I ran over there, and it was Todd."

"Did you think he was dead?"

"No, just passed out."

"Why were you so sure?"

"Ms. Meade, you know as well as I do that if you live in Delmarva for very long you'll learn to tell the difference between dead and passed out right quick."

"Did Mr. Linn look like he might have passed out because he was beaten up?"

"No. He wasn't bloody."

"So what did you do?"

"I ran back home and got a quilt to put over him so he wouldn't get the 'epizootics'. You never know what kind of germs you can get from bug bites."

"I thought epizootics were diseases of animals," Judge Barton interjected.

"Maybe it means that to an *away*, Your Honor, but around here it means like chills and fever."

"Proceed," ordered the judge.

Dana Meade continued, "Did you notice anything else unusual?"

"Well, Monty's car was there, but Todd's truck wasn't."

"Do you know what happened to the truck?"

"In this town, the last one standing takes the car keys from the guy who passed out and gocs around town blowing the horn and stuff to let everyone know he won the drinking contest."

"Objection," barked Ms. Meade.

"Ms. Meade, unless there is a ventriloquist in the courtroom, I believe that you asked the question. You cannot object to the answer of a question that you asked. If you do not wish to know the answer to a question, simply do not ask it," was Judge Barton's astringent reply.

A small titter of laughter rolled through the courtroom. Many of the spectators had only come to get a break from their regular, unexciting routine.

Judge Barton did an about-face, marched to the bench, rapped her gavel and called, "Order, order – proceed."

"The prosecution has nothing else to ask this witness at this time, Your Honor," Dana Meade said and took her seat at the prosecution table.

"Defense, you may begin cross-examination," stated The Honorable Judge Barton.

Knowing that Juanda Tipsword was a well-liked young woman in the community, Farleigh Mullanphy, the defense attorney, did not want to turn the jury against his client by hammering her with cross-examination. On the other hand, he could not allow Monty Tipsword, the defendant, to accuse him of not mounting a vigorous defense against the charges, so he decided on some softball questions for Juanda.

Mr. Mullanphy found it somewhat difficult to refer to the witness as "Ms. Tipsword" since she was a lifelong friend and classmate of his daughter. Several times during his questioning, he had to catch himself from calling her "Tipsy." This was his daughter's nickname for Juanda, but it quickly spread in a less-than-flattering way to the other locals.

"Ms. Tipsword, are you sure that the incident you witnessed was on July 21, 2000," started Mr. Mullanphy.

"Yes."

"Why are you sure?"

"Because most parties are on Saturday nights and they're on the docks. This one was on Friday, and it was at Monty's trailer."

"Are you sure that you could see clearly?"

"Of course – I've spent lots of nights on fishing boats hauling in catches in the dark. I have no trouble seeing at night."

"Are there any doubts in your mind that you have correctly identified the subjects at the party?"

"No doubts! Like I said, these were people that I grew up with, worked with or went out with. I knew everyone except the one guy that I said was built like Monty only he walked different from Monty. Even if I didn't know his name I knew that I had seen both him and Monty at the trailer."

"Have you seen the mystery man around town since the incident?"

"Never."

"Could you identify this stranger from a picture line-up?"

"I doubt it because I didn't see his face. But if you walked a bunch of guys through this courtroom with their backs to me, I'll be willing to bet that I could ID him."

"Your Honor, I have no further questions of this witness," said Mr. Mullanphy.

An idea flashed like a strobe light in Dana Meade's mind. If Juanda Tipsword could positively identify Reynold Barr as being the person present at the party, it would make the prosecution's case that much stronger.

"Prosecution, do you wish to cross-examine the witness?" asked Judge Barton from the far corner of the courtroom.

"Your Honor, if it pleases the court, I would like to take Ms. Tipsword up on her challenge of identifying the mystery party attendee."

"Objection!" called Mr. Mullanphy.

"Would both sides approach the bench?" requested Judge Barton, taking another of her rare occasions to actually be seated.

"What is your objection?" Judge Barton asked Mr. Mullanphy.

"This was not in the prosecution's pre-trial outline of the case," stated Mr. Mullanphy.

"No, Your Honor, it wasn't," responded Ms. Meade. "But when Mr. Mullanphy raised the question it gave me the idea. It was not my intention to bring a surprise upon the court but since the defense's question led to the challenge being made; I think it's reasonable for the court to allow the challenge to play out."

The judge asked, "How long would it take you to set up the scenario?"

"Please give me a five-minute recess. I'll get four men from the gallery, along with the defendant and our mystery man, Mr. Barr. I'll have them walk past the witness stand in such a way that the witness, Ms. Tipsword can only see their backs. We will have her call out their names before they turn to exit the courtroom."

"That sounds reasonable to me. Objection overruled. Bailiff, have the jury leave the courtroom and have them ready to reconvene in ten minutes."

Ten minutes later, court was back in session.

"Ladies and Gentlemen of the jury," Judge Barton said from the far right side of the courtroom, "we are now going to conduct a test of Ms. Tipsword's ability to identify people by looking only at their backs. This is to help establish whether or not her testimony as to the attendees at the party at the defendant's trailer is credible."

Dana Meade thought to herself:

"Oh no, that's not the real reason, It's to establish that my witness was at the party. How strange it is to get the defense to voluntarily strengthen the prosecution's case."

"We will walk five people past Ms. Tipsword so that she cannot see their faces. She will then attempt to identify the people before they are allowed to face her."

The Honorable Judge Barton took a seat on the bench. "Will the first person to be identified please approach the bench without looking anywhere except straight ahead at me? she ordered.

A young man walked slowly to the bench without showing his face to Juanda. "Ms. Tipsword, who is this person?"

"Willie Joe," answered Juanda.

"Sir, are you Willie Joe?" queried the judge.

"I am Your Honor," he replied.

"You may leave the courtroom. Thank you," instructed the judge.

Dana Meade repeated the process, and Juanda correctly identified the two other men. Then Mr. Barr entered the courtroom. He walked to the bench in his curious rolling, side-to-side gait.

"That's the stranger that I don't know. He definitely was at the party." Judge Barton dismissed him.

"Have the final subject approach the bench," ordered Judge Barton.

As soon as the final subject passed her, Juanda called out, "That's Monty. See, they look about the same when they're standing, but they have a lot different walks."

Judge Barton instructed Monty Tipsword to resume sitting at the defense table. "Let the record show that Juanda Tipsword was able to correctly identify by name, four of the five people who participated in this reverse line-up. The fifth person was unknown to her, but she made a positive identification that he was at the scene of the alleged incident."

Under the prosecution table, Dana Meade gave a small fist pump. She had heard in law school that the famous early twentieth century attorney Clarence Darrow had a technique for getting the jury to internalize a crucial point by pausing for a long drink of water while standing in profile to the jury. Ms. Meade arose and utilized Mr. Darrow's technique before saying, "Your Honor, I have no further questions of this witness."

"Ms. Tipsword, you may stand down."

This stand down slightly confused Juanda, but the bailiff opened the gate to the jury box and motioned with his other hand toward the back of the courtroom. As she made her way to the rear door she thought to herself:

"So that's what 'stand down' means. And these *aways* think I talk funny."

"Your Honor, I would like permission from the court to vary from the plan I had put forth," requested

Prosecutor Dana Meade. "Due to the unavoidable delay on Monday, the trial is off schedule. My next witness is Dr. Cunard Lee, the neurosurgeon who treated Mr. Linn before his death. He will be unable to schedule being in court tomorrow so even though this is not in a logical order, I'd like permission for him to testify next."

"Does the defense have any objection to Dr. Lee testifying now?" asked the honorable judge.

"No, Your Honor, we do not," responded Farleigh Mullanphy, counsel for the defense.

"Bailiff, call Dr. Lee to the witness stand," instructed the judge. Dr. Cunard Lee was duly sworn, and the trial proceeded.

"Dr. Lee, you are a neurosurgeon who practices at Neptune Medical Center, is that correct?"

"Yes, it is."

"On Sunday, July 23, 2000 you were called to treat Mr. Linn, is that correct?"

"Yes."

"Do you have your notes from Mr. Linn's hospitalization with you?"

"Yes, and may I add something?"

"I assume that it has a bearing on this case, so yes you may," responded Ms. Meade.

"In this case, I can only speak from what is in my notes. I never saw Mr. Linn when he was conscious, so I never had a conversation with him. Over the years, I have seen many people who were not conscious when I arrived and, unfortunately, never regained consciousness. I am sorry to have to say this in front of Mr. Linn's loved ones, but if I did not have these notes, I would have only the faintest recollection of treating him. This fact is not due to my not caring about him. It is just that I never had a personal relationship with Mr. Linn since he was unable to speak, blink his eyes or even grip my hand."

"Thank you for that difficult statement, Dr. Lee," Ms. Meade responded. She continued, "Dr. Lee, how long after the incident did you record these notes?"

"I did not make these notes. They are the actual hospital records. The only parts that I added were my progress notes and orders written during, or as soon as possible after each episode of care took place. I only retrieved these notes from the medical records department of Neptune General after I received my subpoena for this case. I have made some notations on the papers, but the originals would still be available from the hospital."

"Dr. Lee, how long after you received the call from Neptune General did you arrive at the hospital?"

"About fifty-five minutes. We are required by hospital protocol to be available within one hour after being summoned. During that time, I also ascertained that the emergency medicine specialist had given appropriate orders for Mr. Linn. I spoke with the hospitalist on duty and explained my standing orders in the event Mr. Linn's condition changed while I was en route."

"Did you make any changes to the ER doctor's orders during this phone call?"

"No, the ER staff and I work very closely together. They know the tests that I need and how I like my patients to be set up for surgery."

"When you made your initial examination of Mr. Linn did you notice any exterior signs of trauma?"

"Not really trauma, but there was a small area of bruising on the right side of his forehead. It looked several days old."

"What test or tests did you order?"

"As I said before, I work closely with the ER staff. By the time they first contacted me they had already ordered a CT scan. This is the most important thing that I need to have done, and the results were waiting for me when I arrived at the hospital. The CT showed a 4 x 4 cm frontal contusion with intra-parenchymal hemorrhage"

"Could you give us those results in a little more plain English, please?"

"Sorry, I was reading from the notes. Mr. Linn had a bruise about an inch and a half by an inch and a half on the right front of his brain. There was also some bleeding into the brain itself."

"Were there any other tests that showed potentially dangerous data?"

"Yes, Mr. Linn had a condition known as Marfan's Syndrome. This causes people to be very tall, and among other things, they often have a damaged aortic valve in their heart. After a mechanical valve is implanted in the heart, the person needs to take a drug called 'warfarin' for the rest of his or her life. This is because the mechanical valve increases the risk of blood clots forming around it and being pushed out into the body. The test to determine if a person is getting the correct amount of warfarin is called the International Normalized Ratio or INR for short. The correct level for an aortic mechanical valve is a matter of opinion, but is generally considered to be somewhere between 2.0 and 3.5. When Mr. Linn was admitted, his was 4.3."

"Dr. Lee, could you elaborate a little on the significance of an INR of 4.3?"

"In my opinion, 4.3 is higher than you would want to have when you are about to operate on someone's brain. I suspect that if you or I had a 4.3, we would be walking around with no consequences. However, if you or I had some kind of brain injury, with an INR of 4.3 we could be in the same unfortunate situation as Mr. Linn was."

"Can the high INR be reversed?"

"Yes, but it is not accomplished quickly. I consulted with a cardiologist about the risks and benefits in a patient with a mechanical aortic valve."

"What was the result of that consultation?"

"That the bleed into the brain was the more important problem. We had to do something about that, and soon, or the patient would die."

"Where does that leave the heart valve problem?"

"Lower on the list of problems. Reversing the effect of warfarin increases the risk of a valve-related blood clot, but death from this is not as inevitable as death from bleeding into the brain."

"In other words, we will cross that bridge when we come to it."

"Exactly."

"What did you do next?"

"I started the process for the craniotomy – drilling a hole in the skull to let the blood out of the area around the brain."

"Could you explain to the court why this is urgent?"

"Yes. When there is bleeding into the brain or the surrounding area, you are packing fluid into a closed space. The skull is not going to crack open by itself to let the blood out. So the only thing that can happen is to squeeze the brain. When this happens the blood vessels in the brain get flattened, and blood can't get through. Without blood to the brain, a person has a stroke. If the stroke gets large enough, it will stop the brain from working – the person is what we call 'brain-dead.' There is extremely minimal hope of ever regaining consciousness and practically no hope of resuming the ability to walk or talk. This is why we had to begin the brain surgery without being able to wait for the warfarin to be reversed. Mr. Linn had almost no hope of living if we had waited any longer. He had only a small chance of living even if we started the surgery right away."

"And he did become brain dead eventually?"

"Yes. Eventually, his mother was able to come to the hospital and give permission to stop life support measures."

"This is what is commonly called 'pulling the plug?'"

"Yes, but it's far more complicated than unplugging a toaster. In most cases, death is not instantaneous."

"Eventually, Mr. Linn did die after this was done?"

"Yes, there was just too much brain damage by the time we were able to operate."

"The prosecution has no further questions of this witness," Ms. Meade stated.

Judge Barton spoke next. "Usually at this time of day I would call for a lunch recess. However, Dr. Lee is a long way from home, and it does not seem reasonable for him to be forced to wait while we eat lunch. Mr. Mullanphy, can you expect to cross examine the witness sufficiently and still allow us to recess for lunch and for Dr. Lee to be dismissed in a timely manner?"

"I think I can, Your Honor," Mr. Mullanphy replied.

"Good," stated Judge Barton, and she strode across the courtroom. "The defense may begin its cross-examination."

"Dr. Lee," Mr. Mullanphy began, "you said that it was unlikely that a person with an INR of 4.3 would have a bleed into the brain. However, that seems to leave open the possibility that it could happen. Is this true?"

"Yes."

"Have you ever done surgery on anyone who had no obvious cause for bleeding inside the head other than the INR was elevated?"

"Yes, I can think of two patients."

Mr. Mullanphy took a long drink of water – he presumably had heard the Clarence Darrow story too. "Dr. Lee," the defense attorney continued, "the autopsy report said, and I quote, 'He has multiple healing bruises with various colors around his axillary regions, upper arms, both hands, right flank, left lower back, mid back, lower back, left upper thigh, in the groin area and right shin.' Can you think of any reason other than a beating why Mr. Linn's body would have these bruises?"

"Yes, there is a quite simple explanation. One of the tests to determine a person's level of consciousness is to look for a response to painful stimuli. The simplest way to do this is to pinch the patient, and the less they react, the lower their level of consciousness. Mr. Linn remained unconscious for several days before he passed away. He was likely pinched numerous times. I pinched him several times myself. He was more apt to bruise because of his elevated INR, but over the course of several days the sites began to heal. These were small bruises, not those of a size commonly seen in a beating."

For good measure, Mr. Mullanphy took another long swig of water before saying, "The defense has nothing further, Your Honor."

"Ms. Meade, does the prosecution have anything further," asked Judge Barton.

"Nothing, Your Honor."

"Dr. Lee, you are free to go. For the rest of us, court will reconvene at two o'clock."

This triggered a replay of yesterday's charge on Pickett's Pub. Today Judge Barton was not disturbed about being last in line. If court did not reconvene at exactly two o'clock, she knew that the entire town would understand why. She also knew that if she ate before some of the others, it might cause an awkward situation when court could not reconvene because they hadn't gotten served yet. She watched the interactions of the locals and enjoyed her lunch.

When the court reconvened shortly after two o'clock, the bailiff summoned Jeanette Linn to the witness stand. At this point, the mother of the deceased's own health was in a critical state. She was in a wheelchair, having had her right leg amputated from the ravages of diabetes, and required oxygen therapy around the clock. Her dear friend, Virgie Worthington-Meade, served as Jeanette's attendant, and remained at her side on the witness stand to assist Jeanette during her frequent coughing spells. The bailiff affixed a microphone around Jeanette's neck so that her testimony could be heard.

Dana Meade began, "Mrs. Linn, what we need to do this afternoon is to establish 'what' happened to your son, Todd, and 'when.' We know that this will be painful for you, but it must be done to obtain justice. At any time, we can take a break for any reason. May we proceed?"

In a barely audible whisper Mrs. Linn said, "Yes," and nodded her head.

"Juanda Tipsword has testified that on a Friday evening during July, 2000, there was a party at a trailer owned by Monty Tipsword and that your son was there. Is that also your belief?"

"Yes." This was followed by a coughing spasm and Virgie wiped Mrs. Linn's lips.

"What time did he come home that night?"

"I don't know. I didn't see him until about noon the next day. He came downstairs then." Mrs. Linn broke down in tears. Virgie comforted her.

"What did he tell you at that time?"

"He said that he had been jumped by three guys who hit him over the head with a tire iron. Then he went back upstairs to his room." There was a copious outflowing of tears, coughing and sobbing. Finally, she managed to whisper that she never saw her son alive after that.

After a brief recess, Dana Meade again addressed Jeanette Linn. "Mrs. Linn, what took place on Sunday?"

"I didn't see Todd. I tried to call to him, but I guessed I wasn't loud enough for him to hear me. My friend, Virgie came over and got me up. She wheeled me into the living room. There were these strange tracks on the carpet. Then we noticed that the waste can from the kitchen was in the living room. It had several pieces of cotton with blood on them and some other medical-looking trash inside." She paused again to regain her composure. "I asked Virgie to go up to Todd's room and see if he was there, but he wasn't."

She sobbed, her chest heaving. "Virgie called the Challenger County Ambulance and asked if they knew anything about Todd. They said that he had been flown to Neptune General during the night."

"What happened next?"

"Then Virgie called Neptune General, and after about half an hour of getting transferred from person to person, they told her that Todd had checked a box on his admission form that said that he did not want any information given out about him. They wouldn't even confirm that he was still there or if he was still alive."

"Did you go to Neptune General after that call?"

"No. I didn't have the strength to travel. I wasn't as bad as I am now, but I couldn't do it. Besides my physical condition, my husband Frank's death brought back too many memories. I just couldn't do it – especially since they wouldn't give me any information." She paused again to compose herself.

Dana Meade continued, "And on Monday you heard nothing?"

"Nothing."

"What happened on Tuesday?"

"I got a call from someone saying that they worked for the court and that they wanted to confirm that I was Todd's mother. I asked them why they wanted to know, and they said that the hospital was working on some type of court order. I thought that

Todd had broken some law, so I didn't ask any more questions. Later, I got a call from a social worker at Neptune General saying that Todd was in terrible shape and that his doctor wanted to talk with me. The doctor said that I needed to come to the hospital as soon as I could if I wanted to see Todd alive. Of course I made arrangements to go." Again, Jeanette Linn broke down in tears.

Judge Barton called for another ten-minute recess. When court reconvened Jeanette Linn began her testimony about allowing Todd to be taken off life support.

"What options did the doctor give you?" asked Dana Meade.

It was a leading question and Farleigh Mullanphy, the defense attorney, was within his rights to object. However, there is such a thing as going too far, and the defense chose not to exercise its right. Everyone was aware that Todd Linn was dead and hammering his dying mother was not likely to save his client from a conviction.

"They told me that he had an almost zero chance of ever regaining consciousness. I was told that he might live even if I pulled the plug. It seemed that he needed all of the tubes and drains to live, but nobody knew how long he could survive without them. Turns out that Todd died a short time later. I have never believed that your life should be measured by how many times your heart beats. What's more important is what you can absorb and contribute while you're alive. If Todd couldn't enjoy life or contribute anything to other's lives then why should we force his heart to keep beating? I'm not going to be here much longer, and I couldn't take proper care of him if I was, so I decided that it was in his best interest to stop his life support and as the doctor said, let nature take its course."

"Your Honor, I have nothing further for this witness," declared Dana Meade.

"Defense, you may cross-examine the witness," intoned Judge Barton, still pacing the courtroom.

"The defense has no questions," stated Farleigh Mullanphy.

"Mrs. Linn, you are dismissed," said Judge Barton.

"Prosecution, you may call your next witness."

Hillary Hedgpeth took the witness stand and was duly sworn. She was the lead Emergency Medical Technician when Todd Linn was transported from Delmarva to the heliport where he was flown to Neptune General Medical Center.

"Ms. Hedgpeth, were you present on July 24, 2000 when Todd Linn was transported by Delmarva EMT Services from his home to the emergency heliport?" asked Dana Meade.

"Yes, I was."

"What did Mr. Linn tell you was the reason for his requiring medical assistance?"

"That he had been hit in the head with a baseball bat."

"I have no further questions of this witness," stated the prosecutor.

"Defense you may cross-examine the witness."

Farleigh Mullanphy began, "Ms. Hedgpeth, is this your signature on the bottom of this form?" He showed her the EMT record of the incident.

"Yes, it is."

"There is a line that says 'HEENT.' Could you please tell us what that means?"

"It stands for Head, Eyes, Ears, Nose and Throat. That's part of our physical assessment of the patient."

"Behind where it says HEENT you have written 'WNL', what does that mean?"

"Within normal limits."

"He says that he was hit in the head with a baseball bat, but you judged his head to be normal. Could you explain that?"

"There were no cuts, bruises or abrasions on his head. His eyes appeared normal. In fact, you will also see on that form that I noted 'PERL.' That stands for pupils equal in size and reactive to light. It means that his eyes were functioning normally. There were no visible problems with his eardrums, and his nose and throat were not obstructed."

"In your career as an EMT, how many people have you seen that you were absolutely positive that they had been hit in the head with a baseball bat?"

"None."

"The defense has no further questions, Your Honor."

"Prosecution, have you any further questions of this witness?"

"Thank you, Your Honor, the Prosecution does."

"Ms. Hedgpeth, do you think that Mr. Linn could have been hit in the head by a baseball bat?"

"Objection. The witness disqualified herself as an expert when she testified that she had never seen anyone hit in the head with a baseball bat."

"Sustained."

"The Prosecution has no further questions, Your Honor."

"Ms. Hedgpeth you may stand down. Court is adjourned until tomorrow at nine o'clock."

Judge Barton made her way over to Granny Pickett's B&B, wondering what the elderly lady was going to fix for supper that night. She was met at the door, not by Granny, but by the waitress from last night at The Crab Palace. The suspicion that the waitress and Granny were somehow related was confirmed.

"Granny isn't feeling well, so she asked me to fix you something tonight."

"Got the epizootics, has she?" asked the judge trying out her knowledge of the local dialect.

"No, more than likely just more of the punies that she's been having all week."

"What are you going to fix, Miss?"

"I'm never going to be even pert near as good a cook as Granny. But when I worked over at The Mud Pit they made me cook sometimes when the regular cook was too drunk. I know how to make a soft-shelled crab sandwich and 'cold slaw.' Figured I'd fix them."

The Judge thought to herself:

"Oh Lord, if The Mud Pit falls as far short of its name as The Crab Palace did then I'm probably going to wind up with the epizootics or the punies or maybe even the ptomaines."

Picturing a bar with mud wrestling she asked, "What is The Mud Pit?"

"One of those places where guys take their monster trucks and race through the swamp. Once they get enough beer in them and mud on them they don't care too much about how the mutton tastes."

"Well, Young Lady, I haven't had a beer, and I'm not muddy."

"Don't let that put one worry in your head, Your Honor. I'll get you a beer. But Your Honor's going to have to make your own mud," she laughed uproariously. "I'll have your supper ready in half an hour.

Thirty minutes later, Judge Barton was seated at the dining room table and was presented a plate with an open bun on which was what appeared to be a breaded and deep-fried crab – shell and all, accompanied by one small bowl of tartar sauce and one of cocktail sauce. Rounding out the meal was a generous serving of cole slaw and a tumbler of local draught beer.

"Am I supposed to eat the whole crab – shell, pincers and all?"

"Sure enough – it's a soft-shelled *she* crab."

"How do you know it's a *she*?"

"The guy on the dock said it was, and I didn't see anything to shift my brain," roared the waitress again.

Judge Barton giggled and bit into the sandwich. It was surprisingly good. When she had finished, she inquired as to breakfast.

"Granny figured that I could fry up some scrambled eggs, bits of ham, and boil up some grits. And if I'm real careful I won't even burn the toast. What time would you like it, Your Honor?"

"How about seven o'clock? Will you make some coffee too?"

"Goes without saying!"

"Sounds like a fine mess of mutton," Judge Barton tried the local Chesapeake Bay dialect again. Before she left, the judge slipped a five dollar bill under the edge of her plate. Since it would go on her expense account, the judge figured that it was the least that the good people of Challenger County could do for this hard-working young woman.

Wednesday morning came, breakfast was served, and the judge was off to the courthouse. Court reconvened, and the next prosecution witness, Reynold Barr was sworn in.

Dana Meade began, "Mr. Barr, how did you happen to be in Delmarva on July 21, 2000?"

"I was crewing on the fishing boat, the 'Queen of Buzzards Bay' out of Massachusetts. We blew a water pump and put in to Delmarva to get a new one. Cap'n Marlin Frisch found one and worked overnight to get it replaced. I ain't much of a mechanic, and there was only room for one other person in the engine room, so he told me and the rest of the crew that he wouldn't need us that evening. None of us had any money and most just decided to catch up on sleep in their bunks. I didn't have any wheels and didn't know anybody in town. I was just sitting there when this other ship makes port. I noticed that one of the deck hands looked a lot like me, so I thought maybe I could scam him into believing that I was a long-lost relative. I waited until he came ashore and then I hailed him and asked if there was any action that I could walk to that night. He laughed and said that you can walk to anywhere in Delmarva. He told me to walk up to Swigs Liquor Store, pick up something to drink and then keep walking till I see the trailer park. When I turn into the park, I should keep walking until I come to the last trailer on the left. That's his place. He says things would get started around dark."

"Did you go?"

"Yes, Ma'am."

"How did you buy the beer without any money?"

"I didn't go to Swigs. I waited until I got to the party, and then snatched someone else's six-pack that was next to the cooler. Nobody seemed to notice."

"How many people were there?"

"I don't remember exactly. I didn't know anybody, so it didn't matter to me. It was probably around twenty if I had to guess."

"Do you see the man who invited you in the courtroom today?"

Pointing at Monty Tipsword who was seated at the defense table, he nodded his head and said firmly, "Yes, Ma'am, he's sitting right over there."

"Were there any fights at the party?"

"Not until the party was breaking up. Even then it was more of a shoving match than a fight."

"Who was involved?"

"That guy I just pointed to and some big guy."

"Could you describe the big guy?"

"Yes, Ma'am, he wasn't seven feet, but he wasn't much shy of it. And judging by some giant tuna I've seen on fishing boats, I'd guess he weighed over three hundred."

"Anything else that you recall?"

"Yes, Ma'am, the host-guy called the big guy 'Toddler'. I thought it was funny because if a guy that size was only a toddler, he sure enough would've been a pain to his mama when he was born."

No one reacted to the mystery *away's* attempt at humor, but everyone in the courtroom startled in their seats when Jeanette Linn let out an agonizing scream. Judge Barton poured a glass of water and instructed the bailiff to take it to Mrs. Linn, who nearly choked trying to drink it.

Judge Barton thought of admonishing Mrs. Linn for the outburst but could see no worthwhile outcome of such a move. When order was restored, Ms. Meade continued her questioning. "Can you describe what happened during the fight or shoving match?"

"Well, Ma'am, there was only three of us left – me, the host-guy and that big guy they called Toddler. The big guy said something to the host-guy about nearly getting his hand ripped off by a fishing net. They called each other a few names but nothing serious. The host-guy wanted to get Toddler out of his place to so he could end the party. Me – I had no place to go but back to "the Queen," so I was just hanging out. We all pretty much had a bellyful. The host-guy gave Toddler a shove toward the door. Toddler must of passed-out right then because he just flew down the steps and landed in a pile of wood chips. I didn't see him move after that."

"So Mr. Linn, the one you call Toddler, never touched the defendant, but Mr. Tipsword, the one you call host-guy pushed Mr. Linn out of the trailer and he fell down the steps."

"Yep – yes, Ma'am."

"Why didn't you call 9-1-1?"

"'Cause I just figured he was passed out. It was only three steps, and he landed in wood chips. It wasn't like he hit a rock or anything like that."

"What did you do then?"

"The host-guy and me drove around for a while, and then he let me out at the docks. I boarded 'the Queen', and by morning, Cap'n Frisch had the ship up and running, so we set back to fishing. I never laid eyes on this place again until after Mr. Mann bailed me out in Denver and brought me here."

District Attorney Meade had no further questions for the witness. However, Farleigh Mullanphy requested that the defense be allowed to postpone cross-examination of the witness until it fit better with some of the upcoming testimony. The request was granted. Mr. Barr was allowed to stand down.

The prosecution called Dr. Herman Heller, an expert in the use of warfarin. The swearing-in and establishment of credentials were routine. Prosecutor Dana Meade began her questioning. "Dr. Heller, how many patients taking warfarin have you seen in your career?"

"Thousands."

"Do you agree with the American College of Chest Physicians guidelines that a person with a mechanical aortic valve with no complicating factors should have a target INR of 2.5 with an acceptable range of 2.0 to 3.0?"

"Yes, and I might add that I was a member of the committee that recommended that range some years back."

"Do you agree that Mr. Linn's medical records show that this was probably an appropriate range for him?"

"Yes."

"We know that Mr. Linn's INR was 4.3 when he was admitted to the hospital. What would you expect with an INR of that magnitude?"

"First, let me say that an INR of 4.3 in a patient who was maintained on a constant dose of warfarin would ordinarily be no cause for much alarm. Simply holding a dose is usually all that is needed. However, if that person were to suffer some head injury, an INR of 4.3 could become significant. It could cause bleeding into the brain."

"Could being pushed down stairs, even if it were only three stairs, and landing in a pile of wood chips be enough of a trauma to cause bleeding into the brain with an INR of 4.3"

"Yes."

"The prosecution has no further questions, Your Honor."

"Defense, you may cross-exam the witness."

"Thank you, Your Honor. Dr. Heller, what could cause an INR to go shoot up to 4.3?" asked Mr. Mullanphy.

"I don't consider an increase in the INR from 3.5 to 4.3 'shooting up'. There are many small things that might cause the INR to increase to that level. The most common seems to be not eating one's usual diet. We all need some Vitamin K in a healthy diet. This works against warfarin so what we try to do in warfarin management is to maintain a balance between the effect of Vitamin K in the diet and the dose of the medication. We know that Mr. Linn was injured on Friday night and remained relatively inactive until his hospital admission on Sunday. If he continued to take his warfarin on Friday and Saturday but did not feel well enough to eat like he normally does, this could cause the INR to increase. It also could be something as simple as taking an extra dose of warfarin. Many times when patients can't remember if they took their scheduled dose, they, or a loved one will say, 'Better to take an extra than to miss a dose.'" Juanda Tipsword fidgeted in her seat in the courtroom.

Dr. Heller continued, "We know that Mr. Linn consumed a considerable amount of alcohol on Friday evening. Alcohol and warfarin are metabolized by the liver in much the same manner. The body seems to select metabolizing alcohol before warfarin, so the interaction could have caused the INR to be even higher than 4.3 on Friday or Saturday. There is just no way of knowing because there is no record that he tested on those days. Further, his autopsy showed that he had fatty changes in his liver. When this happens, the person is not able to metabolize warfarin as efficiently so his INR will tend to increase if the warfarin dose stays the same."

"Thank you, Doctor. Is it correct that the fatty changes in Mr. Linn's liver were due to alcohol consumption?"

"Without more history, I cannot be positive. There are other causes for fatty changes in the liver but alcohol consumption is the most common one. We do have a history of considerable alcohol consumption here."

"Dr. Heller, how much experience do you have in treating patients who have fallen down stairs while taking warfarin?"

"I have either been the primary physician or consulted in over one hundred cases over the past ten years."

"So you are an expert in falls associated with warfarin."

"Yes – there may be a few other doctors who have seen as many cases as I have, but only a few. I have published a paper on this subject that is frequently cited in other published articles."

"Could you summarize your findings for us?"

"Yes. More than half of the people taking warfarin who fell down stairs and hit their head died within the next few weeks. Many people delayed seeking medical treatment for their injury for three days to one week. In many cases, it was difficult to determine that people actually fell down stairs because they appeared confused and told many conflicting stories as to how they were injured."

"How did you finally determine that they had fallen down stairs?"

"Mainly from the family members who brought them to the Emergency Room. They had either witnessed the fall directly or were told by eyewitnesses what had happened. It seems strange, but few people were truthful with EMTs, ER staff, or physicians about their falls."

"Do you think it's possible that they were embarrassed about falling?"

"Possibly, but I think it's more related to the after-effects of the fall."

"Had most of the patients consumed alcohol?"

"Here again it is difficult to determine because few people came to the hospital soon after the incident. We've gotten very few relevant blood alcohol levels. However, according to the history given by family or friends there usually was alcohol consumption. But we have little objective evidence such as a blood alcohol level would provide."

"So, doctor, would you say that Mr. Linn fits in almost perfectly with the characteristics of patients in your study?"

"Yes, he had consumed alcohol, fell down stairs, didn't seek medical attention for about three days, and told three different versions of how he was injured – none of which was borne out by independent confirmation."

"Could he have been bleeding into his brain before he fell down stairs?"

"It could have happened that way, but it does not seem very likely."

"Thank you, Doctor. Your Honor, I have no further questions."

"Does the prosecution have any further questions for the witness?"

"Just one, Your Honor."

"Dr. Heller, did you see anything in the records that would have ruled out the allegation that Mr. Linn was pushed, and that was the cause of his fall down stairs?"

"No."

"I have nothing further, Your Honor. Further sayeth the prosecution naught."

Challenger County is in one of the oldest states in the Union and court tradition still called for some rather flowery language.

"Defense, you may call your first witness."

Monty Tipsword was duly sworn. He had considered buying a suit for his court appearance, but later thought better of it. All of the jurors knew him – most since childhood – and he figured that if he got too dressed up it might make somebody think he was guilty and trying to fool them.

It was Farleigh Mullanphy's turn to go first with a witness.

"Mr. Tipsword, did you have a party at your trailer on the night of July 21, 2000?"

"Yes."

"Was Mr. Linn there?"

"Yes."

"Had there been harsh words exchanged between you and Mr. Linn just a few days before?"

"Yes."

"Then why did you invite him?"

"Well, if I didn't invite anybody that I had harsh words with, I'd been drinking alone instead of having a party."

A titter of laughter arose from the spectators.

"Order!" called Judge Barton without halting her continual pacing.

Mr. Mullanphy continued, "Did you exchange harsh words at the party?"

"Not really. Toddl… I mean Mr. Linn was still piss… I mean unhappy that I didn't help him when he got his net caught on a peg, and I didn't let go of my side to help him. He wasn't really up on fishing, or he would've figured out right away that if I dropped my side to help him we'd a lost all the fish. Then, none of us would a gotten paid, and Cap'n would've been out a lot of money for the trip. We'd have all gotten fired and had slim to no chance of getting hired by any other cap'n any time soon. So, while Mr. Linn was starting-in with me again at the party, I pretty much ignored him."

"So you didn't argue?"

"No. I think I told him that if he wasn't happy he could surely find the door. Those are the strongest words I recollect using."

"What happened as the party was breaking up?"

"There was only three of us left – me, Linn and the guy I saw on the docks. Linn was pretty drunk, but I thought he'd drive the stranger back to his ship. I was just trying to get them to leave. Mr. Linn headed for the door, but he was so tall that he knocked his head on the top of the door frame. Didn't draw blood, but it probably stung like almighty. That caused him to stumble backwards and crash into the window a/c. He nearly knocked it plum out of the window. Then he took like two giant steps – you know lifting his knees real high – while he was trying to duck out the door. He got out of the door and then I guess he passed out right at the top step. He crashed down the steps into a heap in the chip pile there."

"Did you push him?"

"Wasn't no need. He passed out on the top step."

"Did Mr. Barr, the stranger from the docks, witness this?"

"No, Sir, he was in the piss... I mean bathroom."

"Are you sure Mr. Barr didn't witness this?"

"Sure I'm sure. If he had seen it he wouldn't have had to ask me what happened, would he?"

"So you are one hundred percent sure that Mr. Barr did not witness Mr. Linn hitting his head, staggering backwards into the window air conditioner and then passing out on the top step."

"I'm not one hundred percent sure – I'm two hundred percent sure."

"Did you call 9-1-1?"

"For a guy passing out? You got to be kidding. Who's going to pay the ambulance bill and all that stuff? Besides, if the EMTs got called every time someone passed out in Delmarva, they'd never get any sleep."

A coughing epidemic broke out in the gallery, eliciting a sharp look from the honorable judge, who was trying awfully hard not to smile.

"What did you do?"

"After Barr got out of the head, we borrowed Mr. Linn's truck and some cash to get a pack of cigs from Swigs. Then I gave Barr a ride back to the docks. Blew the horn real good too, 'cause it was the first time I'd ever seen Linn pass out."

"When you got back home was Mr. Linn still there?"

"Yes. Had a blanket over him. I figured it was Juanda that had done it. Her place was dark all evening, so I figured she was watching it all."

"Then what did you do?"

"Went to bed."

"Further sayeth the defense naught," intoned Farleigh Mullanphy.

"Prosecution, you may cross-examine the witness."

"No questions, Your Honor."

Farleigh Mullanphy rose from his chair, "Your Honor, I'd like to call Mr. Barr back to the stand."

"Request granted, please bring back Mr. Barr."

Reynold Barr went back to the witness stand. Judge Barton stood directly behind the bench and addressed her remarks to Mr. Barr. "Remember, sir that you are still under oath to tell the truth."

"Yes, Your Honor."

Mr. Mullanphy began, "You testified that there was a shoving match at the end of the party, but Mr. Tipsword testified that you were in the bathroom. How do these two scenarios fit together?"

"Well, I was in the bathroom, but it sounded to me like a shoving match."

"You didn't actually see Mr. Tipsword shove Mr. Linn, did you?"

"I er–uh guess not."

"No further questions, Your Honor."

"Court will recess for ten minutes after which we will have the summations of both the prosecution and the defense."

Court resumed after the break.

Mr. Mullanphy rose to his feet, "Your Honor, if I may speak?"

"Go ahead."

"I'd like to make a motion for a summary dismissal of this case. The prosecution has not proven that Mr. Tipsword is guilty of second degree murder."

"The court feels that that decision is best left up to the jury. Prosecution, please begin your summary."

Dana Meade rose to present the summation of the prosecution. "Ladies and gentlemen of the jury, you have to decide how a person of a fairly young age lost his life. You have heard testimony that there were angry words exchanged between the deceased and the defendant while they were working on the "Challenger," a fishing vessel. You have heard testimony that the deceased and the defendant were both present at the defendant's residence on a Friday night. You have heard testimony that the defendant's cousin, who was also the girlfriend of the deceased, did not attend the party because she feared that there would be a fight. You have heard testimony that there was indeed a fight between the deceased and the defendant. The outcome of this fight was that Mr. Linn ended up unconscious in a pile of wood chips at the foot of the stairs of the defendant's residence. You have heard testimony that as a result of this fall, Mr. Linn became confused and did not seek medical help until early Sunday morning. By this time it was too late to save Mr. Linn's life.

It is my hope and indeed the hope of the people of Challenger County that you will conclude that this is second degree murder. Thank you very much for your diligent efforts in making this a fair trial."

Dana Meade returned to the prosecution's table and sat down.

"If it pleases the court, the defense will now present their summation."

"Proceed," said the judge.

Farleigh Mullanphy rose and strode over to a position directly in front of the jury box. Ladies and Gentlemen, you have heard testimony that Mr. Tipsword *MAY* – and I emphasize *MAY* have been responsible for the death of Mr. Linn. However, in order to convict the jury of this serious crime the prosecution must prove that Mr. Tipsword *DID* – and I emphasize *DID* directly cause the death of Mr. Linn. Now I want to point out the features of the testimony that should cause you to have reasonable doubts as to Mr. Tipsword's guilt. The incident that started all of this was several days prior to the party, and while it brought an exchange of what is commonly called 'trash talk,' it did not result in any physical fighting. There was no conclusive evidence given that there was a physical fight on Friday, July 21, 2000 at Mr. Tipsword's party or anywhere else for that matter.

Mr. Linn had a mechanical heart valve, and that required him to take warfarin, a medication that can cause bleeding into the brain. He had a tendency toward bleeding that was increased by several factors as two doctors have testified. He did, in fact, die from bleeding into the brain that might have happened whether he hit his head or not as he was leaving the party. Mr. Linn consumed a large quantity of alcohol as a matter of habit and especially on the night of the party. That coupled with his medication could have caused bleeding without any visible external injury.

The key witness for the prosecution changed his story from seeing a fight between Mr. Linn and Mr. Tipsword to hearing what he thought was a fight. Ladies and gentlemen, these facts plus the doubt about the truthfulness of the key witness should not cause one of you to have a reasonable doubt about Mr. Tipsword's guilt – it should cause all twelve of you to have a reasonable doubt about Mr. Tipsword's guilt. It is not the job of the defense to prove that a person is innocent. It is the job of the prosecution to prove beyond a reasonable doubt that the accused is guilty. The evidence given by the prosecution simply does not prove guilt beyond a reasonable doubt. Thank you all for your sincere deliberation in this case." Mr. Mullanphy returned to his seat at the defense table.

Judge Barton took her seat on the bench. "Ladies and Gentlemen of the jury, these are my official instructions to you as jury members. I would like to thank both the prosecution and defense for strictly adhering to the rules of evidence. Neither side has attempted to insert anything in the record that should not be there. Everything that you heard during this trial may be considered as evidence. You are free to assign whatever importance you determine appropriate to any evidence provided. When you are in the jury room you should discuss any evidence among yourselves. You may not discuss anything about the trial or any thoughts of guilt or innocence with anyone except another member of the jury while you are in the jury room. You must not attempt to hear anything whether in person or via the media about the trial. If you do overhear anything either by accident or in person, you are to inform the bailiff immediately.

As you know, I consider this to be a most unusual trial where there are so many potential conflicts by blood, marriage or friendship. Both the prosecution and defense, as well as each of you individually, have assured the court that you can make a fair decision in this case. The court expects every one of you to adhere to that assurance. Make every honest attempt to come to a unanimous decision. If you cannot make a decision this afternoon, I will give you further instructions as to how you will conduct yourselves over the weekend. Your first order of business is to elect a foreperson for the jury. That person is to guide the deliberation and announce your decision to the court. Bailiff, please escort the jury to their deliberation room. Court is adjourned until the jury announces to the bailiff that it has reached a decision."

The jury convened, and when all were seated, Juror #1, Clementine Tipsword was the first to speak. "I nominate Juror #7, Airak Meade as jury foreman,"

All of the other jury members called out, "Aye!"

Airak was always seeking an audience, so he readily accepted. "Before we go any further, we've got to make double sure that we don't screw ourselves out of those sandwiches. Phoebe billed the good people of Challenger County for that mutton, and it's our civic duty to make sure it gets eaten. We're not having any discussion about the verdict until after we eat."

"Aye!" responded all of the jury members.

The bailiff brought in the lunch and all fed at the public trough. Meanwhile, at Pickett's Pub, the public was paying cash for their food. Alex Everly Mann was sitting at the bar alone when he was approached by Sherriff George Pickett, who patted him on the shoulder and said, "Hope there are no hard feelings. Whatever the verdict, you're welcome to come back to The Charge this evening for a little get together."

"I think I'll give it a miss. I don't want to be here when you people feel free to go after the *aways.* I'm going to try to catch the last flight from Baltimore back to Phoenix."

"It wouldn't be as bad as you think."

As Alex returned to his sandwich he thought:

"Probably worse."

Back in the jury room, there was a good deal of informal deliberation taking placc. On one side the jurors said things like: "Boy that mystery witness sure backed down didn't he? Couldn't tell the truth if his life depended on it. Monty always was a punk, but he ain't no killer."

On the other side the jurors' comments were: "I don't know about Monty – he can be down-right ornery. Tipsy probably knows more than she's telling. Mrs. Linn ain't so bad."

"Yeah," reminded Airak, "everyone's entitled to their own opinion. Let's be fair about this."

A few of the jurors asked, "You think all the folks at The Charge have had time to finish their mutton?"

"Close enough. Let's start deliberating like we're supposed to do."

The bailiff cleared away most of the lunch dishes.

Airak continued, "I'm going to go around the table and ask each one of you what you think. You can just say guilty or not guilty, but you can also give a reason if you want to." He started with the first juror on his left. After the voting was complete, Airak said, "Well, it's unanimous – let's let them know we're done."

The bailiff was called back in and was told that the jury had reached a verdict. The bailiff hustled over to The Charge and notified the judge. The honorable Judge Noble Barton announced to the patrons that court would reconvene in thirty minutes. The jury need not have worried about the trial attendees not having time to eat lunch.

Court reconvened in the usual manner. "The court recognizes the chairperson of the jury, Mr. Airak Meade. Has the jury come to a decision?"

"We have, Your Honor."

"What is that decision?"

"Not guilty. Further sayeth…"

The announcement of the verdict was interrupted by Jeanette Linn's scream, "Justice?" as she fell from her wheelchair, dead on the courtroom floor.

Epilogue

One month after the trial
Denver, CO

Alex Everly Mann and Huyen Nguyen were having dinner at the Bao Dai Restaurant. Over the promised bowl of pho, they discussed the trial of Monty Tipsword.

"I couldn't have concluded this investigation without you, Winnie."

Winnie nodded, "But it's too bad that the conclusion resulted in Mrs. Linn's death."

"Yeah, I'm sorry that it ended that way too. But look at it this way; she was staring death in the face. I doubt that the trial shortened her life by very many hours. Even if she had lived, she would never have accepted the verdict. Jeanette Linn would've died with physical and emotional pain no matter what."

"I still hate that it happened."

"Talk about hating what happened, I really feel responsible for your losing your job."

Shortly after the trial, the Colorado Pharmacy Board gave Winnie her unconditional release, citing repeated insubordination, threats and intimidation of her superiors, abuse of authority, misuse of department resources and law enforcement databases, neglect of other job responsibilities, and case tampering.

"It was probably time for me to move on anyhow. Being an entrepreneur is in my blood. I wasn't feeling fulfilled working as a bureaucrat. Look at the positive side, I didn't lose my pharmacy license, and I'm free to do what I please."

Alex asked, "And what do you please?"

"Some of my classmates are in supervisory positions around the state. I'm going to call them to see if they need part-time help. I have a dream, and I don't want to get bogged down having to clock-in day after day, year after year. I'm free. I could never have said that if my mother hadn't insisted that we flee from Vietnam."

"Do you want to tell me about the dream?"

"It could turn out to be a nightmare, but I hope that you will call me if you land another investigation. I enjoyed the adrenalin rush of going to the jail and convincing Rebar to work with us. By the way, do you know what happened to him?"

"I bought him a first-class ticket to San Diego. I know another retired pharmacy inspector there who became a PI. Joe's problem is that he is too clean-cut, so he doesn't fit in a lot of situations that he needs to check out. He agreed to give Rebar a try at being his associate. I figure that this is probably Mr. Barr's last chance to grow up."

"That's great. I hope it works out for him."

"What about your plans?"

"I'm thinking about taking my computer skills on the road. I'd like to do consulting for companies that want to upgrade and integrate their data systems."

"I think that sounds great. Who better than you to spread around your IT expertise?

"Well, the need for computerized information for patients who get prescription drugs is about to increase exponentially. I'm thinking about contracting with the major pharmacy software companies to produce that information in other languages. I know of pharmacists right here in Denver who are fluent in Vietnamese, Korean, Chinese, Spanish, Farsi, Arabic, Amharic, Igbo, and Thai. Who knows how many others are out there? We could translate the available programs into these languages and work out the characters."

Alex smiled warmly at Winnie. "I don't know how many of my old contacts are still around, but maybe some of them are in top, decision-making positions now. If you trust me, I'll make some calls."

"I'll always trust you, Alex."

"Me, too."

Made in the USA
San Bernardino, CA
23 September 2013